Home Free

2750330

By Cathy Enlow

Printed and Bound by Harold's Printing Co.
Brookings, S.D. 57006

ISBN 0-615-13197-2

Chapter 1

Some people never quite perfect the knack of the furtive look. Holding the head still while looking out of the corner of an eye is beyond them. They don't see things they aren't looking at directly, don't concern themselves with other existence. They turn their heads and their bodies to face what they want to see. It's not that their eye muscles or joints don't move like they should, that kind of thing might be corrected. It stems from a frame of mind, a sense that they are alone, invisible, that no one out there will be caring what it is that they are up to. It's something that's learned early when they are first let out in the world to play.

For Humphrey Dixon this meant that he never learned how to cheat off a neighbor's test, never saw the spitballs coming, never had a crush on a girl that he could keep secret and never got away with any mischief without a lookout.

The beach was essentially deserted with an occasional dog and runner visible in the distance. The road was out of sight, twenty feet above him at the edge of a rocky cliff. There was a turnout ahead where he could see a couple ardently making out on the hood of a car and the point that curved out to sea was far behind him, getting smaller. It reminded him of a site that recurred often in the old Perry Mason series, usually filmed in blue filter to simulate night. They frequently ran a car off that cliff, a little plywood car that made the cliff look much higher. Yeah, this could be that place.

Humphrey Dixon, walking above the tide line, turned around for the eleventh time. A strange, achingly prolonged dance to any casual observer, but there were none of those, not as far as he could tell, for he was frantically looking for the glint that, in the movies, always reflected off the lenses of an observer's binoculars. He desperately needed to be sure that there was no one watching, no one near enough to hear. No one at all, but especially not the Fool.

Humphrey was an observer by trade, not a hunter. Outwitting a watcher was new to him, discomforting, a skill he didn't want to perfect. He knew he could have protected himself better by enlisting the help of his friends, but he'd needed to do this alone. If there was danger, a long conversation with himself had told him that his soul would not have been aided by endangering others and diluting the responsibility. On a less cerebral level he wanted to feel he had the guts to deal with this without rallying the support of a gang. There were guilt and humiliation factors as well, but they were conveniently downgraded.

He knew that the cell phone he held, the one he expected to ring at any moment, was not secure. If the Fool had the right equipment, expertise and determination, he would be able to listen in on the call from anywhere in Redondo Beach. Humphrey knew this. Humphrey preferred to believe the Fool was smarter at legwork than brainwork, so he watched for that glint off his lens. Selective paranoia.

To the north there had lately been torrential rain, floods, mudslides. The ocean was choppy; the clouds on the horizon would probably turn bright pink in a few hours. By Sunday it would rain here. Early January temperatures in the 60's were comfortable but the cold gusts off the ocean caught him ill prepared in Dockers and an old gray football jersey, and the chill heart of those gusts would shiver through him as they passed. When he turned away from the wind it blew wavy strands of hair into his eyes which he didn't notice because of the cold fabric suddenly plastered against his formerly insulated backside. The plan was for him to take solace that there was no one here to interfere, but isolation suddenly seemed idiotic and foolishly exposed. He saw himself as if from a nosegunner's sights, the only target on the beach. He'd give it ten more minutes before he looked for another safe place, a scene change, action to match the storyboard his mind had become comfortable thinking in.

Storyboards, his most useful tool, are renderings used mainly in the film and television industry to augment the script. They show sketches of the scenes and specify the angle, scope and movement of the shots. When Humphrey's mind conjured up a picture, whether from memory or imagination, it was framed with notations about the position of the seer, the direction of impending movement, unusual sounds or lack thereof. He saw them there already, so all he had to do was write it all down.

The message that brought him here had been that he should expect a call between 3 and 4 so he had the opportunity to pick the site for this scene. As time wound down he wished he'd gone for less drama, maybe a bathroom with the water running, a staple of the spy genre. When the phone rang Humphrey stomped around looking for a comfortable place to sit. Every choice was a cold seat, but sitting seemed oddly comforting; made it feel private.

"Mase! Thanks for getting back to me. I won't even ask where you are now and I'm sure you're busy so I'll make this quick." Hum hoped the slight chattering of his teeth would not be misinterpreted as fear. "Do you still have that place in the boonies? You told me once you kept a house out in some town on the plains." He was speaking quickly and knew he must be sounding crazed, maybe it was all just the chill.

"Sure do. Brookings, South Dakota. Nice little place. Good for unwinding. I don't get there much anymore." Humphrey found himself smiling in spite of his bummed mood, as though he were suddenly shielded from his present gale. It was good to hear the voice that used to wake him for his 7:30 class and talk him into inane stunts. He remembered how Mason would run across campus screaming for Humphrey's attention only to whisper the details of some great scheme he needed help with. Like that time they broke into the art lab and stole the nude models wrap-ups. Whenever anyone wondered what kind of idiot would steal robes from people who didn't particularly mind about being seen naked, they snickered conspiratorially. Clearly no one else got it which tickled them no end.

"Good for hiding?"

"Yeah," he answered hesitantly, "Free, you in trouble?"

"Trouble? Nah! I don't want to believe this guy is really a danger. The last thing I should do is give him the impression that he's scared me off, but I'm tired of messing with him! I'd just like to not have to deal with him for a while, get some work done. In fact, my agent..." this sounded good, he should have opened with this line, "...is insisting that I do something so that I can work and make her some money."

"Hey, back up. What guy?" Humphrey stopped fingering designs in the sand and looked out over the waves. The designs were all turning out to be weapons anyway; tendril-like nooses, long bladed daggers, grenades.

"Have you heard of the movie "Wreckage"? About a guy who lets people believe he died in an accident and goes off to avenge some wrongs? Stars Anthony Edwards." He remembered the previews he'd been shown of the movie poster and the spectacular scene of the ferry sinking which would be the focus of the commercials even though it had little to do with the rest of the story.

"Sure. Is that yours?" His voice grinned in associated ownership.

"Yeah. Well, this fall I started getting calls from some fool who thinks I wrote it about him. He says I blew his cover and he wants my ass."

"Don't kid yourself, your ass was never that good. You mean he wants to sue you for stealing his story?" The prospect of his old friend facing a legal dilemma was clearly amusing to Mason.

"No, he says he wants me dead, not able to tell anyone who he is." Humphrey pictured himself being found tied to a chair in his own dining room, the unfortunate finder inching around him, calmly focusing on the duct tape effectively sealing his mouth, the look of complete bewilderment in his eyes and the single drop of blood trickling from the bullet hole in his forehead.

"But if you don't know who he is..." The damp was soaking through Hum's pants and finally hitting skin, time to stand, time to pace, time to gesture meaningfully with his free hand, time to let his fears out for a short breath of fresh air.

3

"Right. But he doesn't believe me. Maybe he really did let people think he died. And I don't think he'd be this upset if it was just that he was dodging child support or a bad credit rating. I think he came back and did something big. And maybe he was getting away with it until the movie and now he's afraid the cops are going to come looking for him."

"But the movie isn't out yet, is it?"

"Mase, this is Hollywood. Upcoming movie plots are widely published and discussed."

"But didn't you originate it?"

"Yes, I did. Listen if it isn't an adaptation it's identified by the plot. Like Connery's working on a comedy about a janitor or Roberts is busy on a thriller about a cancer cure lost in a resort buried in an avalanche. It's all part of the hype."

"So you think he's serious, like a real threat?" Humphrey sighed, feeling that he finally had confirmation that he wasn't just babbling. His shoulders dropped, his free arm fell to his side.

"He's called about a dozen times. Lately I let the machine pick it up, but at first I actually talked to him, tried to tell him that I knew nothing about him, that I made it up and worked on it for months, but he doesn't listen. He won't tell me anything that I can use to convince him he's wrong. The thing is, I really don't know who this guy is, what he looks like. But he's got my number, he might know my address. He could be a nut case who's imagining all this, but that wouldn't mean he's any less dangerous and he could strike at any time. Do I risk having him mow down everyone in the Olive Garden just to get me?" Humphrey stopped to breathe, exasperation sweeping the shivers out of him. "Shoot, whether he's for real or just a nuisance, I just don't want the hassle. I'm thinking that if I just get away from him, he'll move on to something else and leave me alone."

"That is too bizarre! Sounds like stalking. You know LA cops have a strong history with stalkers. They've learned to take them very seriously. Maybe you should report it."

"I did. They tapped my phone for a while but the messages they got were fairly innocuous, not like his usual spiel, not enough to charge him with anything even if they could find him. The trace always led to pay phones. I think he knew they were listening." He kicked at the sand. First it was just to turn over a small shell with his toe. Then to grind the shell into the featureless sand. Finally to nudge it up on a mound and kick it, as if he could send it through the goal posts made by the stacks on the cruise ship halfway to Hawaii, as if doing so would herald a new reality wherein this stuff wasn't happening.

"Possible. You could change your number."

"No. I'm a screenwriter; I've got to be accessible. Lots of people who I want to hear from have my number. Not everyone knows who my agent is, although Jodie

4

says 15% of hard to find has got to be better than 15% of dead." Humphrey could just imagine Steven finally calling the number he'd left with the Amblin' rep and getting a disconnect message. He'd walk out into this cold and choppy sea before he let that happen.

"I see your point. Whatever. You're welcome to use my place. I have no idea when I'd be getting back there and given the weather, I would probably have passed it up until summer anyway."

"Why, what's wrong?"

"Man, I thought you writers kept up on things. This winter is record cold and thick out there. You could probably hole up there until June and not see anyone." Humphrey pictured a scene from fifty feet in the air; a vast whiteness unbroken by trees, sky to match, and in the middle a small log cabin, snow two feet thick on the roof, smoke spiraling up from the chimney, no sign for miles around of any other habitation, the faint trill of a harp wafting in and out on the wind, a kind of Gold Rush without the mountain cliff.

Mason's voice grew reflective. "Actually it would be very attractive as a hiding place. I pay this guy to check regularly for damage and to shovel the walk or mow the lawn, whichever. The utilities are paid automatically by the bank, my car's in the garage. You can probably still wear my clothes." Hum flashed on a door opening on the dorm room they'd shared, ankle deep in clothes. Interchangeable, at graduation they couldn't remember who owned what.

"Have you let yourself go?"

"No!" Mason's tone was a subtle blend of indignant and wounded, a masterful performance in one word.

"Then I can wear your clothes. Cab from the airport?" The snow picture changed to include trees in the yard near the house, which had spread out to include a garage, a street with a huge mailbox, other houses visible far in the distance.

"Airport's in Sioux Falls, an hour away." Picture adjustment: western town with half a dozen buildings huddled together. The viewer rises to a third floor height, turning to see how the one road going through town trails off toward oblivion. "Better you should arrange for Conveyance to pick you up. It's a local service that makes runs back and forth on demand. Information can get the number."

"No cabs?" A horse and buggy ambled past the house in his mind, the two time frames shuffled together, then a string of pickups of various sizes loaded with hay bales, some souped up, some decrepit. "So has this place of yours got electricity?"

"Idiot. It's a regular three-bedroom house in a regular neighborhood. Brookings is a nice town. The largest university in the state is there so they are not without culture. There are supermarkets, malls, cable."

"What about clubs?"

"Ah, well, sorry Free, country western rules." Cowboys in boots, dusters and big hats hopped out of the pickups parked at a typical truck stop. "Plenty of bars but you'll probably want to go down to Sioux Falls for jazz."

Humphrey stopped his pacing and let the chill envelop him once more. "Maybe this isn't such a great idea."

"You've gotten to be such a snob in your old age. Think of it as an extended camping trip and you'll be pleasantly surprised. You used to like to rough it."

"I used to own a teddy bear." Humphrey saw himself standing outside an outhouse in a snorkel hooded parka clutching a worn blue panda in the crook of his elbow, computer in the snow beside him, cord sniffing the ground like a puppy, the faint harp tone being nudged by the thrum of a bass.

"You still do. When do you want to go? I'll mail you a key. Once you're inside you can use everything as though you were me."

"ASAP would be great. What about the people? What should I tell people who are suspicious at seeing a different guy around?" Hum pictured cop cars squealing to a stop around a house, dozens of people in bathrobes spilling out of neighboring houses pointing at him, demanding, 'What have you done with Mason Landers?'

"Actually that won't happen. When I'm there I just kind of hunker down. I don't go anywhere, I don't see anyone. I don't really know anyone in town. I can't think of anyone except the realtor who can match my name and my face. Even the guy who mows. You could be me and no one would know. And Free... if you write a big bucks movie about this, I want my cut." Hum had to smile at that. He had no idea what the other half of the Mase and Dixon line did for a living, but anyone who could keep a house and car just so that he had some place to chill out couldn't have been doing too badly financially. Mase had been an engineering major. After college Hum had lost track of him for a while and when he resurfaced Mase had repeatedly dodged questions about how he lived. All that his friends knew was that he worked overseas a lot. They'd tacitly agreed to assume that he worked for the CIA and quit asking him.

"Deal. Mase, I really appreciate this. I'll keep track of what I owe you."

"Don't bother. It will be good for the house to have it occupied during this cold thing."

"How cold?"

"I've heard wind chills of 70 below."

"Yikes!!"

"See what I mean, a snob and a wimp." Humphrey disconnected and watched until the snow dissolved and once again the ocean surged toward him. He stamped his feet and brushed the sand off his pants only then remembering to look for signs of someone watching him. Not a soul around. Well, he thought, he didn't have to stay in the boonies if it was unbearable. Unhunching his shoulders, pocketing his phone, he reminded himself he was just a California guy who, to any casual observer, could just as well be out inspecting the surf before he got out his board. Dang, why hadn't he thought of his wet suit?

Chapter 2

"I really believe we have to rethink this thing. Horace Evans could have done it." Despite his assertion, Dan had been shaking his head for three whole minutes while looking at the police case file and continued to do so. It was a conclusion he simply could not evade and finally had to voice. Bobby, in response, rubbed his forehead with such force that the tops of his ears were being pulled forward. There seemed to be an itch in his brain that he was determined to scratch.

"The dead guy?" Bobby murmured. Dan switched to nodding. "You think the dead guy killed our victim?"

Dan switched back to shaking. "I know, I know. It sounds crazy, but it's the only explanation."

"It's no explanation, Dan. The guy is dead. Listen to me." Sitting at the desk facing Bobby's he couldn't easily reach him to shake sense into him and settled for raising his hands in appeal. "Dead now for almost a year. He's a belt buckle being covered by fish shit at the bottom of the Pacific."

"Oh, I see your point, Bobby, believe me. Just hear me out. Let's assume Horace knows he's about to be fired. He suspects the company's found out about his shady dealings, which they did. He's been sent to Indonesia on an impossible assignment knowing that when he fails he's out of there. They won't even have to go to the expense of proving his previous wrongdoing. Suddenly he finds himself on a ferry that's sinking. People all around him are dying, but he's okay.

"'What if...' he's thinkin'"...what if one of these other guys is identified as me? I can walk away.'" Dan paused to let the plausibility of the scenario materialize. "Bobby, nobody has any idea who was supposed to be on that ferry. There were dozens of unidentified bodies, people that nobody missed. If there was no ID found on a body, it just slipped through the cracks of procedure. He could have planted his ID on any mangled body similar to his own and just become one of the hundreds of unidentified survivors." Dan was pleased to see Bobby still listening, although he was not moving a muscle. His evaluation: could have been concentration, could have been a concerted effort not to alarm the patient, a toss up, better charge ahead.

"He waits awhile to be sure that he's in the clear. Makes some quick cash and gets himself back to L.A. Five weeks after he's dead he kills his former boss leaving his own prints as well as a number of conflicting leads. Cops are stumped, none of the leads pan out, he's home free. He starts building himself a new life with a new name, somewhere else." Dan looked around to see that he'd caught the attention of a few others in the squad room. He would rather have been sure that Bobby was convinced before letting the other detectives in on his theory, but he was stuck.

"Then he starts thinking how he'd sure like to get the guy who blew the whistle on him. Hey, it worked before, how often does a guy have a foolproof opportunity for revenge? This time he decides to frame a specific guy, no use letting the second case stay open forever like the first one. And the frame looks real good, doesn't it? It does. Just the one problem that we don't believe Washington did it and he passes the lie detector." Dan gave his partner a pained and desperate look. Bobby broke off eye contact, yawned and leaned back in his chair, arms folded over his belly. The others listening, who hadn't heard all of the premise waited quietly (one cursing when the phone rang and she had to answer it) each looking like they were on the verge of doing something that might fall within their job descriptions.

Bobby judged the timing to be just right for relenting. "So, how do we find Horace?" Dan smiled broadly and judiciously refrained from his usual demonstrations of triumph. "If this guy is out there, and I'm not saying he is, how do you suggest we find him, or haven't you thought that far?"

"I agree that it will be tough, but remember no one did any work on that lead once we found out Horace was dead. He'd be stupid to do so, but he just might have gotten in touch with some of his old friends, or maybe someone who knew him thought they saw him sometime recently when they knew they couldn't have. Basic police work."

"Okay, but we better document this real well. The boss is not going to take kindly when we ask for a warrant on a dead guy."

Chapter 3

"Jodie, I made it." Humphrey leaned back in the living room recliner; a plush and decorous beige. He'd taken off his woefully inadequate and sopping boots in the front hall and the furnace hadn't cranked up enough yet for him to take off his jacket. He had worn his desert hiking boots, the heaviest jeans he had, a plaid flannel shirt over a baby blue crew sweater and an old ski jacket which ended fashionably at the waist, providing an Hercules-like profile but no tush protection. An L.A. kid, he didn't have much to choose from for warm wear and he knew Mase would have left a whole wardrobe at his disposal.

"I had no doubts that you would, Hum." He snuggled his butt into the chair for maximum back support and looked around the room. Facing the recliner was a simple entertainment cabinet with an old 15 inch color TV with knobs and no remote (although it was, indeed, attached to cable) and a VCR with about a dozen tapes stacked at the side. In the corner was a hanging lamp which was plugged into a timer at the outlet. Across the room was a beige brocade sofa and matching chair flanking an end table which doubled as a small set of bookshelves. Even from the recliner he could see some of the titles: Bourne Identity, The Paladin, Hawaii, Jane Eyre, Brain Building. "Any delays? Lost luggage?"

"No. All cut and dried. I had time to check out the airports on the layovers, but not so much that I wanted to get plastered. And just as promised, there was this old guy waiting for me holding up a Mason sign."

"Mason? Why Mason? Are you having an identity crisis?"

"No. But I got to thinking that if I'm going to be using all of Mason's stuff and if, as he said, no one knows him here, it would be that much harder for the stalker to find me if no one here knows Humphrey." He beamed at his stroke of sound reasoning. Looking further around him he saw a bare dining table with four chairs, no hutch. A sliding door to a patio where he could make out stacked lawn chairs under a blob of snow that, through the combined effects of drifting and settling, looked like the Cat in the Hat's hat about to fall over. It struck him that the furnishings were sparse, tasteful, certainly better than a motel room and way better than the Goodwill stuff he might have chosen himself, but lacking, of necessity, the myriad little accumulations of daily living; plants, piles of magazines and newspapers, tables loaded with framed photos and candy bowls, last night's coffee cup, carelessly discarded articles of clothing.

"Hmm. There's some logic to that." Jodie had encouraged him to go but now was feeling reservations due to the lack of control the intervening distance imposed on her.

"Of course there is. When we got close to town, this old man and I, I asked him if he knew how to get to the address I'd given him. He said sure, he'd picked me up there before."

"And what would you have done if he'd said no?"

"Oh." A chill ran through his warming body like he'd been scanned and found wanting. He felt his forehead contracting, the inside corners of his eyebrows rising, his eyes blinking repeatedly, the left side of his upper lip curling upward. Like a Twilight Zone mask, he took on a completely involuntary look of dismay and regret. He knew he had to be more careful in future. In his head he saw Barney Miller's squad room. Wojciehowicz stumbled into the room announcing that there was a break in the case. "Some taxi driver in South Dakota reported a fare who didn't know how to get to his own house. The locals will maintain discreet surveillance until we get there." Everyone grabs a coat and the room is emptied, papers flutter in the breeze made by their quick exit.

"So you think because the old guy didn't recognize the difference between you and Mason, you're home free?"

"Well, I think it's worth the try. Seems like a nice enough town, what I saw of it. It's about as big as it was when I looked it up in the atlas. That hour along the interstate between here and the airport in Sioux Falls, I swear there's only one gas station. There are lots of exits but all the towns are out of sight. The isolation was making me feel a little bummed until I saw that Brookings is right on the highway, a welcome oasis.

"You pass some major industry on the way in, and there's all your regular franchises, lots of trees, malls, lots of new homes being built."

"Is it big enough for stoplights? I remember a cousin from a small town who was so proud when they were deemed big enough for a stoplight." Hum remembered the one street town he'd once thought this place might be. Cartoon stoplights popped up all along the route.

"Yeah, several. There are some big old houses, but the tallest structures are the water towers. There's a golf course and I don't remember seeing anything particularly seedy." He scrambled out of the chair and sock-footed it to look out the front door, his wet pant legs made fwappy sounds as he walked, and he winced when he stepped in a puddle of melting slush. "When I got to the house I had to wade through two feet of snow to get to the door. Mase had hired someone to shovel the sidewalk but not the drive. So before I can look around town I have to go out and shovel. And it's like zero out there." Hadn't Mason warned him that he'd be in for a change in daily functions? He should have remembered that pace and priorities as well as bathroom facilities are altered when you camp out.

Through the door's window he could clearly see his snow path. The old guy had left him at the neighbor's driveway when he saw that it was the only way to get to the sidewalk. A dozen cookie cutter oval holes led to two irregular depressions. One where he'd misjudged the location of the first step up to the door and fell on his face and another where his bag had landed. Unconsciously he reached down to rub the spot on his knee that even now, numbed to Humphrey's consciousness by the cold, was the site of a white cell rally. Later, when he found warmer pants in Mason's closet to change into, he would find swelling and discoloration, the outward signs of subcutaneous party hats and banners.

"Hum? Have you ever shoveled snow?" Did he have a choice? If nothing else he had to obliterate the evidence of his previous bout with ignorance. He would shovel if it took the rest of the day, and it might. The snow he fell in was mighty hard. As he struggled to get his footing he found layers of ice in the snow and thick slabs had been pushed up by his bag, like flows in a more fluid sea of newer snow.

"No. When would I have ever shoveled snow? When you go skiing they've taken care of that." He remembered the ski lodge he'd been to last, a three storey log affair, and imagined some grizzled little old man, broken shovel parts piled up behind him, out in the dead of night sweeping the last vestiges of a three foot snow fall into a dustpan.

"Yeah, so be careful. It can be hard on your back, uses muscles you aren't used to using. There's a knack to it." He imagined a guy in short chinos and brown saddle shoes racing to get his hands on a class schedule at Northridge, looking over his shoulder as he hyperventilates. Paging quickly through the pages he finds the means to his salvation: Shoveling 101, Early European Shoveling 347 and Existential Shoveling 614.

"Well then, I'll just have to take it slow and learn as I go." He turned and went back to what had to be the coat closet. Surely somewhere in the mass of woolen things thrown onto the top shelf Mase must have heavy gloves to go with the heavy boots placed neatly front and center as you opened the door.

"Jodie, have you heard anything?"

"Hum, you just left. No, he hasn't called." Jodie was actually relieved that Humphrey had finally asked about the Fool. To have not done so would have indicated a level of denial she didn't want to have to deal with from far away and limited to iffy cell phone contact.

"Good. Later. I've got a lot of work to do." He reached his hand into the depths of the closet stuff and pulled. Hats, caps, gloves, mittens, scarves, backpacks fell to his feet. He stepped back out of the way and tripped over the boots which he'd already set aside. As he fell back his feet went up catching the mittens and scarves, raining them down on him again and he sure hoped the winter coat Mason had left for him was long enough to buffer his battered buns.

Chapter 4

In late November Cicily Trimble had been waiting for a table at Pepito's on Ventura along with 37 other people in a holding area approved for 25. She'd chosen her waiting place so that the friend she was meeting would be able to see her upon entering. From her vantage point, when not watching the door, she found she was able to read the laptop screen of a guy who undoubtedly didn't realize his vulnerability. She'd recognized within a few seconds that what she read was of considerable importance, that she had to see the rest of it and that should he realize she was watching, she might be in big trouble.

The man was on a private chat line explaining to someone that he'd been assigned to flush out whoever was leaking classified information. Her first reaction was FBI or CIA type classified; national security, international relations. Her little heart pounded as if the love of her life had walked through the door. Or maybe it had something to do with the tobacco industry. There had certainly been a slew of things coming out lately that the big boys were none too pleased about. But the rest of the scrolling lines seemed to have nothing to do with anything like that.

Since the participants in the e-mail dialog knew what they were talking about they didn't elaborate in any way that gave Cicily the clues she needed. Before too long she pulled back, aware that she'd been staring at the screen, an invasion which was obvious to several others waiting. Fearful that she would miss needed information in her efforts to appear nonchalant, she pulled some papers out of her bag and held them so that only a slight shift of her eyes was needed to see the laptop. Thus she was able, before her friend showed up, to glean the names Beetle, Marsh, Bossey Tong Tong and Crenshwind. She repeated them in her head until they formed a song she would remember when she had a chance to write them down.

As a weather girl Cicily didn't have ready access to the information databases at the station. What she had was a sweet smile and a charm that she'd found to be most effective on certain geeky types. She'd been using that charm on Harlon for several months. She'd met him in karate class where he was a very poor but persistent student, and she had used his inside information to get her job. She'd had to sidestep his ardent advances several times, but she'd done so without rancor, because Harlon had three talents; he was passionately suspicious and able to smell out deeply hidden inconsistencies, he took tremendous pride in his ability to access information and he was a fabulous kisser.

She'd heard about his kissing prowess from a fellow karate student, a quiet young man who'd been Harlon's friend since grade school. It did not occur to Cicily to wonder how he knew. Cicily had been skeptical of this report, yet intrigued. With much trepidation she realized that she needed to test this assertion. She approached Harlon without guile and he proved delighted to comply. He may have few social skills, but given the chance to exercise this talent he abandoned all trepidation. Cicily was hooked.

Having been asked for proof on another of his talents, Harlon's first attempts to decipher the four names were disappointing for Cicily. Harlon assured her that he'd keep trying. By the time she'd finished her last broadcast of the day he had something for her. "Crenshwind, I believe, is Crenshaw Waxler Industries. They are a firm of environmental engineers; they do a lot of testing for companies who need to meet EPA standards. Bossey Tong Tong could well refer to an international facilitator named Rosey Wong Tow. She seems to be completely freelance with no ideology whatsoever. Beetle and Marsh I can't be sure about, but in looking for a common factor I checked another environmental related company and found a Marsh and Batelle on the personnel list."

"So what does it mean?" Cicily asked in her most professional demeanor, for she hadn't a clue.

He leaned back and replied with an air of complete indifference, "I don't know."

Cicily, her mouth hung open in a most unattractive manner, stared at him in disbelief. What about his driving thirst for knowledge? His need to get to the bottom of things? What about his need to please her?

Suddenly her eyes narrowed. "You little shit," she seemed to be thinking. After a few seconds her look reverted to its previous innocence, like watching an interview with parts edited out. "Well," she finally said, "who would know?"

"Hm. There's this guy who does clean up work for a different environmental engineer, a much smaller operation. He doesn't owe me anything so he may not want to talk but I'll ask him."

"Good. Good. How long, uh, will that take?" She reached up and fiddled absently with her hair. It was a nervous habit of hers which she had discovered was interpreted by nearly everyone as a sign of boredom.

"Well, I'm not actually sure where he is right now. I think he said he was going to the Star Trek convention in the Twin Cities."

"Oh." Cicily was feeling quite out of her element. Did she want to trust someone who went to a Star Trek convention? And what did she know of environmental engineering? She wasn't going to understand what they were talking about if they did find a connection. And if Harlon wanted a date in payment what was the friend going to demand?

"Well, listen, Harlon, I think it would be best not to foster any suspicions among the middle management types, so don't push on this, okay?"

"Sure, Cic, but I don't think that's a danger, the suspicions, I mean."

It took Harlon and his friend three weeks to come up with a list of names as the possible whistle blower the guy with the laptop had been ordered to find. They had discovered that there was concern in the various environmental monitoring companies that a slight increase in the number of surprise inspections, the specificity of those inspections and the timing indicated that someone who was aware of minor irregularities in the monitoring equipment was tipping off the authorities. Although the list of the people who were probably aware of any one of the problems was several hundred people long, hunch and educated guess had narrowed it to seven. One of the factors they looked at was whether anyone else had already asked their sources about the people they were interested in. Harlon figured that the laptopper would have had a more direct line on the suspects and would have beaten them to every clue. He promised Cicily that he would continue to monitor this factor over time to see if he could pinpoint who the laptopper was still interested in.

Harlon started hinting in January about the date he expected to get and even that a date wouldn't really cover the debt. "You know, Harlon, I'm going to be real busy with this stuff. I'll have to do it on my own time, primarily. I may not want the station to know I'm working on it. So our little date is going to have to wait until this story gets me a promotion."

"Sure." Harlon was confident that it was just a matter of time. After all, he was a computer geek and geeks were the future.

Chapter 5

"Jodie. Great. How's it going out there?" Humphrey peeked through the bathroom window at the front yard and wondered when the snowplow would come through.

"Turn on the news, Hum, it's raining big time. How are you adapting?"

He chuckled. "Adapting? What is this, a science experiment? The domesticated animal returned to the wild? It's just a different climate not another world. This is America; everyone gets to be the same. There may be no Rodeo Drive, but the Pizza Hut is closer. Everything is just closer." He started walking aimlessly.

He didn't want to tell her that he'd noticed so many differences. People smiled and looked you in the eye even when they weren't selling you something. He'd found it threatening until he stood back and saw that they did it to everyone. Another world, an exotic culture? He had friends who would not believe him when he told them that people were known to leave their cars running while they ran into the store for a little something or stopped to mail a package. They would laugh at him for years to come at this foolish raving.

He knew he shouldn't be so cavalier. Jodie was genuinely concerned about him and, being used to having him close enough to shake some sense into, this separation must be hard on her. "Things are fine here. Nobody made a fuss about my 'return'." He wobbled his head and put his hand out splayed for emphasis when he said 'return'. "The car is a '93 Prism and it started with surprisingly little trouble after sitting in the garage for who knows how many months. I stocked up with food and stuff. Mason has an old DOS based 586 that's full of passworded files, but there's enough free disk space for me to work with even if it is just a text based word processor. It's a comfortable house and the people are real friendly without being pushy."

"Tracy called." Funny how she sprang that on him. Pretty Tracy popped back into his head. Her shiny chocolate skin, her hazel eyes, the straight black hair that swung so purposelessly into her eyes. Odd that he hadn't thought about her since meeting the snow. If he'd been longing for the beach, surely Tracy practicing moves in her bikini would have been there, beckoning.

"I broke up with Tracy after Christmas. She said I was no fun anymore, I was taking this Fool thing too seriously. What did she want?" He remembered the casual way she'd dismissed him. The thought of Tracy pleading for his return, hands clasped beseechingly, eyes weighted with contrition, wasn't an unflattering concept to him, if unlikely.

"As I heard it, she left you because she didn't want to show up in your next movie. She'd watched you doing it to everyone else you ever ran into and she decided not to give you any more ammunition." Humphrey didn't reply to that although Jodie gave him several heartbeats to chime in. "Why she called was that apparently she missed you. When she found out you'd left town she got to thinking that maybe there was more to the calls than she'd thought. She wanted to know if you were okay." He started pacing, finding things to straighten up, a coat to hang in the closet, a picture in the entryway to study. If Jodie hadn't heard the ambient noises, she would have thought they'd been disconnected.

"Not where I was? Because you know that could be an angle for the guy. If he was watching me he could have seen me with Tracy and now be using her to track me down." Hum couldn't help but see Tracy tied up in some dank basement, her shirt torn away from a shoulder, a knife held to her throat, the fiend's face hidden by the ceiling in this view from halfway down the stairs. Shadows shifted as the single bare light swung slowly. The faint but steady sound of water dripping could be heard while the Fool waited futilely for Tracy to answer his demands.

"Using Tracy? Is your brain frozen?" Just for a second he'd managed to think of Tracy as a mere female rather than the kickboxing stunt double she made a nice living as. No one had used Tracy since she was 6. "Hello?"

"Yeah, you're right. I'll just assume you didn't tell her where I was."

"Clever guy. She didn't even ask. How's work? Got any ideas yet?"

"For a new story?" Hum felt compelled to watch his feet, more specifically his socks, as he walked around the house. The way his toes spread out as he stepped down was suddenly intriguing. "Jodes, I know eventually you're going to encourage me to use my present situation, but that would be too incestuous. I would feel like I wanted it to continue just to see how it turned out. I'm not going there. I won't."

"Uh-huh." He knew that tone. She would acquiesce now, but in a couple of years, if he was still around, she'd crank up her pearl smooth voice and suggest with perfect innocence that if he really was blocked there was always the stalking of that brilliant and handsome screenwriter.

"I'm working on a couple of ideas. Like, remember when you were a kid and the local TV station had a program where kids would come to the studio and sit on bleachers and they would show cartoons and do little things?" He was still watching his feet and should have seen where he was going but he bumped his head on the doorway nevertheless.

"Little things?"

"Well, it varied. They seemed to have these shows all over the country. Some places they would have a puppeteer, some places it would be a caricaturist, or a folk singer or a clown. These people were idolized by the little kids, became local celebrities."

"Okay." She accepted it even if she didn't remember.

"I'm intrigued by the possibility of one of these people going on to be, oh, like a dominatrix, some kind of closet sexual deviant. Because the personality traits would fit; need for attention, willingness to be humiliated."

"Hum, I think you're mixing up the dominatrix and the victim."

"Okay, whatever. I'm not exactly an expert on this topic. Still, I think it's worth consideration."

"And you're going to research dominatrixes in Brookings, South Dakota?"

He had to pause, had to. While in fact he hadn't considered this idea to the point of planning research, would it really be impossible to find someone here to research? For a few seconds he mentally delineated the steps he would take to find appropriate practitioners; personal in the paper, ad in the doorstep shopper, cruise the sleazy bars, but then let it go. He didn't really want to use that idea yet and the longer he waited the more he feared that Jodie would find it intriguing. "Or... what about whitewater rafting, like the Endless Summer of rafting. I bet there are more people who've rafted than surfed." He stopped to listen to the silence for a while. Jodie obviously wasn't impressed. "Don't worry. Something will gel. There's always that time travel piece I worked on before. Except... I didn't bring any of my notes on it." While rubbing the bruise on his head he studied the contents of the refrigerator, grabbed an apple out of the basket on the counter, but put it back; shouldn't chew an apple on the phone.

"So, tough guy, are you feeling safer?"

"Jodie, I am not here to feel safer. I'm not running from the guy. I came here to get some work done. But I will say that this anonymous thing is working better than I expected. I took his library card over to see if I could check out a couple of books and they didn't say a thing." Although, now as he thought about it, the librarian had looked at him strangely. When she handed him the books he'd just checked out, he asked if that was all. He was used to a more lengthy process. She nodded, but she must have been wondering what else he thought he should be getting. "It's a nice place. Open, modern, well used, good collection for its size. It will be useful."

"So your cover is secure. What about your funds?"

"No sweat. I went to a bank in Sioux Falls. I've had the paperwork sent to the agency to have my royalties deposited directly. I can use a local ATM. As a back up I've bought some traveler's checks under Mason's name using the cash I brought with me."

"So much for your ongoing income, what about your LA holdings? And credit cards? Getting into them might give you away quicker than sweet talking Tracy."

"I won't need to. I can pay for everything I need with cash and the money coming in from the royalties will be enough." He could feel skepticism oozing over the airways. He carried very little cash in LA. Credit and debit cards were accommodated everywhere, why would you risk it? "Really, I've been assured that there hasn't been a mugging here for about five years. I'm telling you Jodie, there are definite advantages here. No suits, no $100 haircuts, no Beemers, no gourmet delis with unrecognizable pieces of food attractively arranged, no one I have to be seen with."

"Not bored?"

"Nooo! Of course, I have yet to be snowed in. Mase was right about the weather. It has been monstrously cold here. But they treat it like some cosmic badge of honor that they carry on despite it. They are currently experiencing their 'regular January thaw'. I believe it got up to 20 and the sun melted these dandy ruts in the ice packed on the streets. They're like four inches deep. And I go to the store and the people are so goddamn happy thinkin' how much worse it could be, even with a quarter of the parking taken up by piles of snow. I haven't had to shovel for almost a week. I actually saw a kid on the street yesterday in shorts." He grabbed a bag of bagels out of the fridge and set the top half in the toaster oven.

Hum could hear Jodie chuckling. Jodie was the only agent he knew who did most of her business on the phone. She had one of the sexiest voices he'd ever heard. He'd been surprised when she put off meeting him during their initial negotiations. He'd come to believe that this indicated that the book didn't match the flyleaf. As it turned out, Jodie was a cutie. She bore, with her curly dark hair, crinkly-eyed grin and cheerleader enthusiasm, a striking resemblance to Rebecca Schaeffer, the promising actress who'd been murdered in the '80s. People in the business remembered Rebecca fondly and tended to see that likeness as a contrivance if Jodie hadn't had a chance to prove herself prior to their meeting. Jodie had proven to be a very effective agent. Her deals were consistently good for her clients and those they worked for. Still, show business politics was often oblivious to logic.

"As long as it wasn't you in the shorts. It sounds like you're settling in. I'll expect some progress out of you by next week."

"Ja wohl!" No way would he have anything that soon. He had to get comfortable being Mason Landers before he could get back to work as Humphrey. A believable portrayal was essential if he were to preserve his own anonymity and safeguard Mason's position as well.

He found so often he was drawn to watching the snow. Clicking off the phone and setting it with the bagels back in the fridge, he wondered why that was. It's not like anything about the snow was changing, some nuance he might miss. It just sat there, sparkling.

Chapter 6

Bobby sat at one of the terminals at the far end of the homicide office. He'd been working at it for almost half an hour while Dan was downstairs. He heard his partner's voice and called out without looking up. "Dan, come look at this. That new movie, "Wreckage", got me to thinking..."

"Yeah, I saw the promos and I thought it was a bit too much of a coincidence, too." Dan threw a file on his desk in passing and waved to the woman he'd been talking to on his way back from Evidence, as she left the room.

"Just for the heck of it I did a term search in the reports database for ferry. You wouldn't believe, by the way, how many cops don't know how to spell." Dan had perched his hip on the side of the desk. Bobby, who looked up at Dan from his hunched position over the keyboard, felt a crick in his back. If this were what he did all day he would demand an ergonomic workstation. In lieu of that he leaned back in the chair, stretched his legs out, flexed his back muscles and thought momentarily of Juanita. She'd been his partner when he first made detective. She would have occasional brilliant flashes of insight. The rest of the time she functioned well doing the grunt work. What kept her there as long as she was was her habit of giving neck rubs to anyone sitting around. She was very good at it, relieving a lot of tension without interjecting the expected touch of sensuality. It was a zone for her. While kneading knots out of temporarily numbed coworkers, she could let her mind focus on other matters. But Juanita was gone now and Dan wasn't a soothing kind of guy.

"There's a report referred from Santa Monica from a guy, a screenwriter, who says he's been receiving threatening phone calls. The caller claimed that the writer blew the caller's cover by writing a movie about someone who survives a ferry accident and goes on to wreak havoc on the gangs who killed his family." Bobby looked up at Dan with a satisfied grin. Dan nodded contentedly and popped his gum loudly.

"Seems the cops up there tapped his phone, but didn't get anything they could use so it's been sitting there. Would you like to do the honors?" Dan took the report and dialed the phone. But there was no answer. He tried the alternate number and got an answering service where he left a message. Dang, now they'd have to wait.

Chapter 7

"Free? How's it goin'?" Humphrey had been shaving when the cell phone rang and he had been tempted not to answer it. It would only be Jodie bugging him again about the work he was supposed to be spending all his waking energy at. What did she know about the time cost of snow maintenance? Checking the freeway report to plan the best route to shave 10 minutes off of a routine 75-minute trip didn't seem to compare with the inconvenience of taking ten minutes to scrape your windshield so that you could make a three-minute trip. He'd learned the advantages of getting up at 6 to shovel the drive before the dog walkers came through and left compressed footprints that messed up his timing when the shovel edge hit them and stopped dead. The jarring this placed on his muscles seemed to him to be worse than when he routinely got hit by a 300-pound linebacker so many years ago.

He'd gotten up early this morning to shovel even though there was no new snow. It was a necessity he had not undertaken gladly. Mason's guy was still taking care of the sidewalk and Hum had shoveled the driveway the evening before once the snow had stopped at 6 inches. He'd heard the plow come through about one in the morning and resolved to get up as soon as he awoke, having learned the week before that the pile left in the drive by the snowplow got harder the longer it was left.

With his first slice into the two-foot ridge he thought about Jodie's warning. He'd chosen not to mention to her how sore he'd been after his first shoveling effort. How had he thought he would put it, ...like I'd slept on a porcupine.' No, he couldn't tell her that and confirm her warning. But since then he'd found it to be a good aerobic exercise and a welcome one since he didn't have Tracy to play with. "Mase? I didn't expect to hear from you."

"I thought I better make sure the house was really fit for habitation. Did you have any trouble?"

"Heck no! It's fine. That old guy picked me up like you said. I did have to shovel the drive..."

"Oh yeah."

"...but once my socks dried and I found the VCR remote I was set." Hum imagined the primitive cabin he'd first pictured and wondered how much more satisfying it would have been if he had really had to chop up wood, haul it in, start a fire with sticks and search the woods for berries.

"Good. They never have, but you never know when the pipes are gonna burst and you have a basement full of water. Or somebody could break in. There isn't much worth taking but if a person had nothing, what's there could keep them cozy for a while. Anyway. Heard anything more about that guy?"

"No, thank God. Of course, if he does give up on me, it just might be that we never hear from him again. You know it would really be nicer if he would send a formal notification. Like: 'So sorry. You were boring so I decided to look for the new "Baywatch" chick. You are hereby relieved of your entrapment'."

"You wish. It would almost be better to draw him out and have the cops catch him."

"But first we'd have to convince the cops that they should be looking for him." Humphrey could see himself forced to take the matter into his own hands, waiting in a darkened doorway, wrapped in a trench coat, shielded by a wide brimmed fedora, ready to spring the trap while Jodie paced seductively in a red silk dress beside the beat up 1944 vintage Jeep which was her personal treat. Sure, the Fool (being a fool) would walk right into that trap. Hum could imagine the vindication he would feel hauling him into the station, duct tape encircling his body from elbow to wrist like a top. It had always worked well in old cartoons.

"Well, right now they're busy with another high profile murder. I suspect your case is just a sticky note. Maybe in time they'll come around. So, you think you might be staying for a while?"

"Yeah, I think I'll be able to get some work done here." Hum surveyed the back yard and remembered how he'd gone to the trouble of moving the computer up from the basement, one piece at a time, cords trailing behind him, only to find that the view distracted him. It was partly his own fault for putting new seed in the bird feeder.

"I'm glad, Free. I sometimes think I should quit and try something I could do from home. Oh, I also wanted to tell you that I won't be accessible for a while. If there's trouble, you can still leave a message with the number you used last, but I won't be able to get back to you any time soon, maybe months."

Wow! He'd gone years without contacting Mason at times, but to actually be inaccessible was kind of creepy. "All part of the job, huh?"

"Yeah."

Hum tried to think of non-classified reasons for being inaccessible for months; rowing up the Amazon, roady for the Stones, research at a polar station, lounge singer on a round-the-world cruise, jail time, sub duty, undercover as a Trappist monk, (oops, no, that would be classified) a real monk, nah, no way.

"Listen, Mase, as long as I have you, what do you know about the university theatre department productions?"

"They're usually quite good. You should go if you have a chance."

"They're doing *Merchant of Venice* now. I thought I'd go tonight."

"Do. I think you'll be pleasantly surprised. I went to *You Can't Take It With You* a while back when I happened to be there. It was perfect casting, best I've seen."

"Well, okay. Everything's fine here, I really don't foresee anything happening. Like you said Mase, it's a nice, peaceful little town."

"I always thought so. Well, must go. Hang in there, Free."

Chapter 8

"Hum, I talked to the cops today." He spit coffee back into the cup, spilled some on his pants and quickly took the still dripping cup to the sink to dump it out.

"Did they find him?" He was so absorbed at hearing the words that he didn't catch the tone of dread in her voice.

"No. These were LA cops. They think the guy who's been calling you might be responsible for a couple of murders."

"Shit! I knew it, I knew he had a good reason for blaming me." The cup ricocheted off three sides of the kitchen sink where he'd thrown it. Whether he'd done so out of triumph or anger was debatable.

"What?" Jodie wasn't sure she'd heard right.

"Oh, you know what I mean. That it was more than just credit he was ticked about. Do they know who he is, where to find him?" Humphrey wished he'd been there to talk to them himself. He was so ready to see them dragging the Fool into the station, his hands cuffed behind his back, his head lowered in shame, his pants in tatters from the dogs that had brought him down, one shoe lost when he'd jumped from Santa Monica Pier, toupee dangling out of his pocket, the air around him ripe with the smell of a lost load.

"What they know is who he really is. His name is Horace Evans. Just like the guy in your story, he was supposed to have died in a ferry wreck, the one in Indonesia..."

"I knew it!" Sweet vindication. Humphrey had assumed that the first calls were some kind of joke. When they continued he'd gone to the library and looked up ferry accidents in Facts on File. There'd been a few in the last couple years, bad ones. He had written most of his "Wreckage" script prior to that so they weren't part of his research. That's when he started believing that the guy might not be joking.

"...so now, like the movie, he apparently has a new identity and they have no idea yet where he might be. They don't have much to go on except these crimes."

"Well, that's reassuring," he said with considerable sarcasm. The police, when he had finally gone to them, didn't sense the danger as he had. But it had gone on for so long without the guy making any move that Hum had halfway come to accept that they might be right. After all those months of looking behind him he'd gotten used to the quiet safety of this frozen campsite. Now he found himself rushing around the house locking the doors and closing the drapes, tripping over the furniture in his haste to secure his fortress.

"So they're going to keep looking for him?"

"Oh sure. Of course. It's part of a murder case now. They're, like, always open." While Jodie's spirit seemed to have lightened somewhat, Humphrey's had dipped deep into the pool of rank possibilities.

"Jodie, are you sure they were real cops? Did they try to get you to tell them where I am?" Hum bit off a corner of a fingernail, something he hadn't done since high school. He stared at his finger and wondered if he was going to need that teddy bear after all.

"They'd left a message with the service trying to get ahold of you. I called them then called LAPD to verify their authenticity and got a description. One of them looks a lot like Dan Akroyd, who was a great Sgt. Friday." He heard Jodie giggle at this apparently indisputable sign of competence and had to shake his head at her efforts to ease the tension. "I'm confident that they are legit. And yes, they did ask where you were, but once I told them you were in seclusion, working, they agreed that that was the best place for you. I gave them copies of all the transcripts you made of the calls as well as the ones to the answering service. If they need any more info from you they'll go through me." Hum stopped in his wandering and literally jumped around, a full 180.

"There have been calls since I left?"

"Uh, yeah." Stupid slip, she hadn't mentioned this to him before and they both knew why. Had they been face-to-face one look would have confirmed that they had each contrived the same scenario. The number Horace had called before now forwarded to an answering service which replied that the party was out of town but they could leave a message. Humphrey Dixon had placed himself beyond the caller's reach. Since they now knew Horace Evans was serious they should expect him to seek the nearest available contact. In professional circles Jodie was listed as Hum's agent and she was the authorized receiver of messages at the answering service.

"Listen Hum, if he couldn't find you when he knew your number, maybe he won't find the answering service. The service never identifies themselves." They were both silent for at least a minute, trying to let that possibility provide them with some reassurance; Humphrey watching the snow fall in clumps of flakes, Jodie watching the lights blink on her phone set. It didn't work. "You realize this blows your theory that he's a prankster and he'll forget about you once you've been away for a while. I hope your friend Mason isn't planning on moving you out."

"No, no, Mase has no plans to come back." Hum was thinking of all the dandy surveillance equipment he's seen while researching a previous film. That was years ago, what they had available today must be real James Bond stuff. "Jodie, even legitimate surveillance can tap into cell phone calls now. These cop guys could be listening to us right now."

Jodie caught the hint of panic in his voice. "Humphrey. Listen to me. They haven't even had time to get back to their office. If you're worried about these cops, I'll use some sources and check them out. Just sit tight and work on putting a story together."

"I have a real bad feeling about this, Jodie."

"Then maybe you should concentrate on something else. Tell me what's been going on."

"Not much." He forced himself to dredge up that short-term memory. "Oh yeah, I saved a kid's life today."

"Ah, just your typical day. So how'd you manage that?"

"Well, I was on my way into the library. Keep in mind that the parking lot is packed solid with ice. Stuff's curb thick. This little girl, oh, about 10 or 11, comes running out. She was looking back at a couple of kids who followed her out, like maybe they were chasing her. Not maliciously, she was laughing.

"So she's not looking where she's going and she slips on the ice and slides. Just then this car drives in. It was going kind of fast to get up the incline of the driveway, and brakes hard to get this open spot but starts skidding, heading right for the kid. So I slide over and scoop her up out of the way.

"When I put her down she was kind of pale and big eyed so I figured she's in shock and any minute she's going to start screaming. I took her back into the library and turned her over to a librarian."

"And you just left?"

"I told the librarian she was almost hit and that maybe someone should be called to come get her. She thanked me and while she talked to the kid I left. I didn't want to have to leave my name."

"Ah yes, the anonymous thing. That must be putting a crimp in your love life. How are you managing without your regular stable to choose from?"

"As though it were any of your business." He took a deep breath. He had a habit of becoming passionately involved with a woman whenever he had a deadline and was stuck for an idea. Usually it was someone conspicuously incompatible. As consuming as that passion might seem at the time, when the plot finally presented itself, the passion was comparably inconsequential. Always, there would be Jodie to point out his folly, look out for him no matter what stupid fix he got himself into. Yes, his love life usually did turn out to be her business.

Hum could feel an hysterical laugh inching up from his gut. Okay, get a hold of yourself. Don't let on or you'll scare Jodie. He squeezed the phone between his cheek and shoulder and shook his hands out violently. Then he grabbed the phone and rolled his shoulders to loosen the neck muscle tension. "I've been to Sioux Falls a few times. Found a couple of nice bars, some good jazz down there. Met a girl."

"Ooo. I knew it. Another one bites the dust."

"Hey! She's very nice. A consultant. Financial analyst for small businesses. She likes jazz. More importantly she doesn't have any interest in talking business, hers or mine."

"So what do you talk about?"

"Talk?" Jodie giggled on cue and Hum could feel the rest of his anxiety subsiding. Pamela had proven in their few encounters to be a very good diversion for him: smart, pretty, athletic, vibrant. All she lacked was an appealing voice. She spoke too slowly, a cadence which contrasted with her high energy level. And there was a slight condescendence in her phrasing, as if it were forever parent's day and everyone was in her kid's first grade class. "We talk about jazz and sports and politics. We do things that don't require talk, like...now watch it!...like concerts, racket ball, flea markets."

"Flea markets?!"

Humphrey knew this would irritate Jodie. "Yeah, flea markets. Jodes, you wouldn't believe the stuff! It's a gold mine!" Hum remembered the huge expanse of tables in the arena filled to the edges with stuff and people roaming from place to place quickly, jadedly surveying the contents, searching for something they'd been seeking or, better yet, something the value of which the owner was woefully ignorant. Much of it was junk but here and there he saw things that would have fit right in to the decors of trendy restaurants, antique shops and the homes of the mighty all over Hollywood. And they were dirt-cheap. Old toys, kitchy lamps, antique implements.

"And this woman, she's interested in this stuff?"

"Yeah, Pam knows all about collectibles. She knows what's hot and what's underpriced. She says they can be a fabulous investment." Hum thought about when she'd taken him to a local antique store and pointed out the things they'd just seen at a flea market. The mark up had been as much as 2000% for some of the most godawful stuff he'd ever seen.

Jodie sensed a possible shift in career choices and there was no way she wanted to be involved with a junk dealer. "I wouldn't know. I'm glad you found someone, Hum. That's good, but you still need to keep working. Not just for me, but because you have a tendency to dwell."

"I do?" He well knew how easily he obsessed. He could never understand why Jodie objected so inasmuch as it all eventually made its way into his work and ultimately benefited her. So what was the big deal?

"Twit." Jodie rarely concluded conversations. She just stepped away from them.

Chapter 9

Dan and Bobby had four cases they were working on concurrently. Two of them were fairly routine; the leads were panning out and it promised to be just a matter of time before things fell into place. One of them was a pain in that there was a connection with drugs which brought them into contact with the drug traffic investigators who weren't too thrilled about being asked to compromise their operation just to get a murderer. The connection was largely a matter of inference and without the connection they had nothing substantive. That case too, was just a matter of time but the time line was longer. The fourth case was that of a businessman who seemed to have been killed by the company driver but they were sure that it had really been Horace Evans and that he'd killed before.

They explained to their Lieutenant why their best bet was to find the guy who was harassing the screenwriter. They firmly believed that he too was Evans. Once they could prove Evans was alive, they could tie him to the two murders with hard evidence and motive. The lieutenant was not in the mood for innovation.

"The writer has left town. His harasser has discovered that the phone is now answered by a service. The logical step for him is to get information out of the service about who is receiving the messages." Bobby, who usually presented their progress in a casual way, knowing the boss was fairly confident in their methods, had chosen to take a decidedly proper stance to this meeting because the premise was so shaky. The boss shook his head as though he were hearing about why his teenage son had decided to carry the leaking garbage sack back from the game on the front seat of his new Buick.

"Look, if he got the guy's home phone number, which is already unlisted, why can't he get the address? Do we know if the writer's home has been broken into?" The lieutenant, like any good lawyer, often asked dumb questions just to be sure they'd been covered. Fortunately for him his squad didn't take his choice of questions as a sign of stupidity. That trap was left for the perpetrators to fall for.

"SMPD report said no and we haven't checked personally. But the caller had been calling for weeks before the writer left. If Evans had the address he surely would have gone there instead of calling. We can check to be sure though." Dan knew they'd come up empty but if the lieutenant had asked, it was likely that the DA would ask as well.

"He could break into the answering service office but there's someone working there all the time. He might have a better chance at sweet talking one of the operators into looking in the files for him." Bobby sheepishly caught himself from perching his hip on the corner of the Lieutenant's desk.

"He might have already done that." Dan thought that had he been planning this crime he would have gotten the writer's address a long time ago. At the very least, as soon as the answering service took over he would have been on that lead.

"Yeah, in which case he would know that the writer's agent, a Jodie, uh, White, is the one picking up the messages. According to the agent, the service wasn't given any idea of where the writer was or is." Shoot, by checking his notes Bobby was beginning to look like he wasn't up to speed on this. Fact was he liked what he saw in the agent, felt comfortable with her and tended to think of her just as Jodie.

"What's his name, the writer?"

"Humphrey Dixon. Wrote that new film, "Wreckage". That's why Evans is after him." Dan smiled triumphantly.

"But the writer's harassment case is in Santa Monica. You want me to authorize my homicide team to investigate a crank call case for Santa Monica?" He shook his head. The Lieutenant knew exactly what they wanted and he knew it was a logical request. He had so few opportunities for humor in this job, rubbing it in about the trouble they were putting him to was a simple indulgence. "Have you talked to whoever is assigned to it from SMPD?"

"Uh, no. We've got the report they last filed in the database. We wanted to clear it with you first. Politics being what they are." Bobby hated politics more than anyone in the department did.

"I taught you well. What's your plan?"

"We'd like to set up a trap at the answering service, but in case he's already been there we should cover the agent because that's sure to be his next stop. If we could be sure that he hasn't been there before and doesn't know the agent or anyone there from elsewhere we could set up a policewoman in her place, but even then there's no way of knowing when he'll make that contact. The best would be surveillance."

"But," Bobby and Dan exchanged a quick glance before Dan continued, "but we know that the manpower for surveillance isn't likely to be approved. We'll need to get her cooperation, of course, on anything we do. She does most of her work on the phone. We could have her talk to him, set up a meeting and have a policewoman there when he comes. Or maybe we can tag her, maybe a direct cell phone connection. We'd have to see what she'd go for, what would work best with her routine, so it doesn't look suspicious. You know."

"Yeah. Okay, hang on until I can touch bases with someone at SMPD. We'll try to make this as inconspicuous as possible."

Chapter 10

It was well past the time Jodie had said she wanted a report on his progress but she hadn't gotten on his case. He knew it was out of deference to his situation but he still felt some personal satisfaction in being the one to call her with his story rather than the usual case of her wringing it out of him.

"Jodie, I've a story for you."

"So, your love life has fizzled, has it?"

"No, it has not. I go down to see Pam whenever I can make it between storms. Sometimes three times in a week."

"Mmm. Gotta watch those storms."

"Like you would know. Even when it only snows a few inches, it blows around for hours afterward, so thick you can't see to drive, you can't make out the edge of the road. And the drifts! Some little town has whole houses buried in drifts. I've got a two foot drift inside the garage where it blew in through the crack under the door."

"And if it weren't for that you'd be at Pam's side, right?"

"I spend plenty of time at Pam's side. There are no complaints."

"Except for the LA girls you left behind. Hum, there are riots in the streets, wails of despair keep us all up at night, the nunneries are filled to capacity."

"Cute." He sorely missed this banter. It was common for Hum to drop by Jodie's office every other day just to shoot the breeze. She might be on the phone but she rarely had visitors. He'd stay 5, 10 minutes seldom mentioning his work. It never dawned on him that this was not her standard procedure with her clients, he just did it that way and thought no more about it. "Jodie, sit back and listen to what I have so far on the story."

"Great. Do I need any props?" She pushed her chair back and carefully positioned her heels on the desk. One of these days she'd look into getting a couch. This wasn't such a comfortable position, but she always felt that it helped to get close to

'Mommy, read me a story' mode when listening to her clients' pitches.

Since she did most of her work on the phone and could make do with a smaller office Jodie had asked for special office furnishings. Since she was good, she'd gotten them. The carpet was a thick Hershey chocolate brown. The wall facing her was brick. Fake brick paneling to be sure, but good quality fake brick. In either corner were tall plants, a parlor palm and a ficus. There was a painting on that wall. She had several to choose from and changed them often. The others resided in a custom built teak box which served as a stand for an intriguing sculpture done by a famous but unnamed client.

She'd had a wide sill built into the window beside her for a variety of plants which acted as a curtain. Below it, protected from sun damage was an antique credenza. She'd provided a forest green wingback chair for her clients because she just liked looking at it.

"No, you twerp. This is a very sweet story, no violence." Hum couldn't help smiling to himself. He was absolutely sure that Jodie didn't have props. She did have cupboards in her office which could hold such things and she would often say to him 'Wait, let me get my gun and see if that works', or 'Hum, I've got my duct tape right here and it's not holding up like you say it will'. People in his stories tended to have guns for one reason or another, some life-or-death conflict. She'd teased him about it for years.

As he began he pictured her listening in her office 1700 miles away. (He'd found a card posted on the fridge giving the mileage to many places away from Brookings.) He thought she probably put the phone on speaker to save her ear. At first he had her resting her face on her arms on her desk to cut out the light and distractions, but decided he liked it better for her to turn completely away from the papers and files to stare at the wall behind her desk which was covered by photos. Maybe close some drapes, orange ones, to bring a nice sunset glow to the room. Perfect.

"Hum, you're branching out, I'm so proud."

"Can it! I believe this concept has a very good chance." He'd typed up a preliminary treatment on the computer, but he greatly disliked reading his pitches. Invariably if he just talked it through something new would come out of his mouth that hadn't been part of the original concept, something the story couldn't do without. He had his notes, but he didn't really look at them. He placed himself in a zone devoid of distractions and walked from room to room at a steady pace oblivious to everything he encountered.

"There's this middle aged woman; widowed, 2-3 kids off on their own. She lives in the house she raised her family in, she goes to the same church, shops in the same stores and meets with the same bridge club, art group and do-gooder groups she has for years. Her husband left her modestly provided for. Her passion is flowers so she opens a little shop on Main Street. (Maybe you haven't noticed that all over the country there are empty stores on small town Main Streets because of the malls.) She calls the shop Bittersweet and specializes in unusual arrangements using nontraditional plant life, not just daisies and roses. Although her work is well received, there just isn't that much business in such a small town. It looks like she may have to bail out, the business is starting to eat into her savings.

"Then she wins a few million in the lottery on a card she has her son buy for her regularly. Rather than make a big deal about it she has her son, a public defender in a big city (who is reluctant because it's completely outside of his expertise) handle arranging for the claim to be made anonymously, in the name of a foundation which he quickly sets up.

"She insists on this, saying she has all she needs and as long as her living expenses are secure, she wants to use the money to do good. She wants to go out and find people genuinely deserving of a break, just a little boost.

"The question is can she find such people while remaining in a quiet midwestern town? Can she help people in her own community without them knowing about it? Can she adequately make the determination of who should get help?

"You hear all the time about people who die and leave fortunes to schools, libraries, hospitals and their neighbors had no idea they were wealthy. It can't be that hard to hide it. But these people don't seem to have been that philanthropic during their lifetimes, so there's no one clambering for their cut. Can you really give a lot of money away anonymously? Can you hear the stories of your neighbors and provide some with relief without someone figuring out who did it?

"I think you can. I think it would take some good acting, some humor, and a good attorney." Hum stopped at a notebook he kept near the recliner and made a few notes.

"I think she should be successful in her efforts for some time. Then I want someone to figure it out, some con man well versed at recognizing angles. He should try to con her out of a modest amount. When he's successful, he tries for a lot more and threatens to expose her operation if she doesn't comply. She gets upset; he thinks she's folding. She lets him proceed as though he'll get the money he wants. He makes commitments, brings others on board. Then she pulls the rug out and he follows through with his threats. He appeals to all the people in town who are in need of the help she can provide but who she hasn't seen fit to help. He's surprised that most of the town doesn't turn on her.

"See he doesn't understand humility. He doesn't understand the joy of anonymous philanthropy. He doesn't understand the value of work, so he doesn't know that people gain self-esteem from work, which is often of more use to them than the living wage they get. These are what the people try to get him to see, but which he leaves town not seeing." He stopped while more notes were made in his notebook.

"Once she's exposed she makes public a report from the foundation which verifies that it's nearly out of funds. Only she and her son know that as soon as she heard from the con man, recognized him as such, she had her son move most of the funds to a new foundation. By the time the statement is prepared, there's no way of telling that the funds weren't all distributed.

"Before he leaves, the con man asks her 'Why did you give me the money in the first place?'

"She says, 'Because you really didn't expect to get the money. You expected me to turn you down and you could make your threats right then. But by giving you the money there was just a chance, a tiny chance to be sure, that you might recognize the possibilities. The people I give money to don't want to have to ask for it, they want to provide for themselves. They've just gotten to the point where they can't. Just a little help will get them back on track and they'll do everything they can to show that they were worthy of that help. A person gets something they didn't earn, they need to make the most of it and pass it on or it's wasted. That's true of looks, talent, knowledge, money. Give and get, get and give.' Ooo, hold on." Jodie was patient while Hum made more notes. "'It's basic physics. For every action there is an equal and opposite reaction. Some folks give before they get, some get before they give. Karma, there's no escaping it.' With that he leaves town and she goes back to her flowers and her secret charities.

"Well, that's it. What do you think?" Hum knew it took a little time to sink in and that the first reading was never as good as it could end up being, but Jodie always tried to give a pitch a fair assessment. He expected her to think on it for a couple of minutes, as she usually did, and to that end had made himself a nice thick sub sandwich. He'd put the phone on the table and, like Dagwood, he sat poised with his mouth open as wide as it could go for the first relished bite.

"I like it," Jodie declared.

"Waa?" was all he could get out with his mouth full and the phone far out of hand. He put the sub down but it all fell apart anyway. "What was that?"

"I like it? Didn't you think I would?"

"I thought you'd think about it." He wiped off the side of his chin and tried to bolster the side of the sandwich, collapsing like a three hour sand castle.

"No need. It has a lot of potential, Hum. I think you're on to something. I take it there's plenty of local color you can glean from your present locale?"

"Well, yeah, I don't want to be too obvious, but you know, there's always a local drunk." Hum pictured his own father passed out in bar booths all over greater LA. The drunk was a character he and Jodie had found he could safely incorporate into any story he wrote. He knew there was a local drunk here, but he hadn't really thought of using one in this story.

"Go ahead, run with it. You have your agent's blessing. Is there anything else?"

"No, I guess not. You don't want to suggest a different angle?" She always, always threw something at him, some unforeseen character to mix up the tightly knit relationships he'd designed, some obscure point of view, some obstructed trait, event or history that would help him to look for more depth in what he'd already deemed plausible, clever and compelling.

"No. I want you to develop what you have. Oh, and send me a copy."

Chapter 11

"Hi, are you the owner of the shop?" Hum had visited all the flower shops in town a couple of times, browsing. Most had been quick runs. He'd grab a cheap prepackaged bundle and be on his way, looking for all the world like a man who'd forgotten a date or needed to beg forgiveness of someone. Most times of the day there were no other customers and Hum felt it was essential that he be able to examine the shops and their distinct dynamics without becoming the focus of those dynamics. He'd found that after work seemed to be the best time for him to hide among other shoppers. So he'd made his after work assessments and had chosen to concentrate on Bascomb's Flowers because there seemed to be a less frantic tone to the customer service. This is how he expected his character to be, since she was more interested in the flowers, in the impact and lore of the flowers, than with the volume of business or the take for the day.

The woman he approached now was the oldest employee he'd seen there and seemed to be the one the others deferred to. She was tall, slim, had gray hair piled up like Katherine Hepburn, held atop her head by an ornate gold clip which appeared worn but not flaked off so was probably real. It worked well with the small diamond stud earrings and simply framed half glasses. None of this elegance looked out of place with the baggy denim overalls and tennies. Perhaps it was the fine, crisp Liberty print cotton shirt that tied the two looks together.

"Yes, I am. My name is Orinda Waters. Is there a problem?" Orinda had a slow, grandmotherly rhythm to her speech. Hum searched for a trace of a southern accent but there was none in what she'd said so far.

He smiled warmly. "No, no problem. I was just admiring your shop. You must have grown up with flowers." He turned around to quickly survey the harmonious displays of plants and flowers. So often, specialty stores tried to fill every spare crevice with examples of their wares; lighting stores with fixtures hanging from every two feet of ceiling; furniture stores with row upon row of chairs, tables, desks; earring stores with aisles of twirling racks dripping with ear bobs. Bascomb's had sections where like kinds were clustered but they were broken up by a table with one centerpiece, a window with one Boston ivy, a recliner with one Parlor palm. They suggested practical uses. They made sense. Humphrey saw the comfort he felt here as an encouraging sign.

Orinda chuckled. "I wish I had. My mother was horribly allergic to flowers and soil molds. She couldn't stand to have any growing things in the house. Actually, I never thought it was as bad as she made it out to be. After all, she could walk across the grass to the car. But she never wanted to take a chance so there was nothing green inside and nothing but grass outside." While she spoke to him she poked her fingers into the nearest pots and determined that a couple of them needed more water. Touch was sufficient. That allowed her to focus on Humphrey and her visions of the past, which seemed to hover near the window.

Humphrey continued to stare at her. It was a habit he was largely unaware of. Some found it disconcerting, others assumed he was listening carefully to their words or to some inner guidance. These pauses while he stared, often followed by a quick and enticing smile, had earned him a reputation as a deep thinker. Although not totally undeserved, in reality he was as often seeing storyboards of auxiliary thoughts. The fact that he responded with appropriate comments or good advice was merely coincidental.

"My father, however, didn't want his children to go without so he would bring us books on flowers and he found this wonderful wallpaper which showed hundreds of plants and their names. When we traveled, he would take us to the public gardens.

"When I got married, I thought I would have my chance but my husband got a wonderful job in New Mexico and for twenty years all I could get to grow were cacti, which can be quite beautiful, but they weren't enough to fill the longing in my soul.

"Brookings has wonderful soil. The climate can vary over the years, but we adjust to it. Did you know the city sits on an aquifer? We have better access to water than almost anyone in the dry years."

"I didn't know that." She was granted one of his most endearing and honest smiles. He would be hard pressed to disguise this woman as the main character in his story. "You seem to have a lot of competition. It must be a struggle to keep the business viable."

"It seems so at times, but I have a lot of loyal customers and there are times of the year when we all do well. We've all been able to develop our own little specialties. Did you have something in particular you were looking for?"

Hum had anticipated that he would have to find something to be buying as a cover for continued conversation. "Do you know the meanings of flowers?" She nodded, a sly grin inched in. "I have a friend who is very modest and shy. Most people don't think of her as such because she's quite lovely, but I know her to be so. What would you recommend?"

"Ah, well, you know that one is fairly logical. First you have your violets for shyness. You remember the old expression: a shrinking violet?" Oh, yeah he nodded. "Then you add the purity of white lilies. One can be, theoretically, shy but not pure."

"Oh, yes, I've run into some of those." Kelley Wislowsky came immediately to mind. She hardly ever spoke and blushed at the most benign things, but with the merest suggestion whispered in her ear, Kelley was all over you.

"Modesty infers purity."

"Indeed. Violets and lilies. That sounds very nice. Would that be too much trouble for you to make up?" She shook her head, a dip in the corners of her mouth, which indicated that it would be a cinch. She turned and went into the back room. Hum let her get started then moseyed over to peek in. There was no one else around although he could hear noises further in the back. "Running a flower shop must be a lot of work. You seem to love what you do." She nodded enthusiastically. "If you had the money to expand, would you do so?"

"You know," she cocked her head to the side and let her eyes roam around the room, "I've never thought about it, but no, I don't think I would. Things seem to fit here. It feels just right. I might fix it up some, a new sign maybe, but I don't think making it bigger would improve it one bit."

"What if someone famous were to endorse your shop and people started coming from all around? You might have too much demand, need more staff, need more room for people to get around."

"That does seem to be what happens. I know of a chocolate factory in Nebraska. Good stuff. Got so popular they had to make the store bigger just so that people could get in the door in winter. I can't see that happening here. Even if I didn't think this was just right, I'd be afraid that once I went to all that trouble people would stop coming. No. I'd find another way."

Humphrey smiled and leaned back against the doorway. "Mrs. Waters?"

"Orinda."

"Orinda, do you believe in karma?" She smiled and returned to her work.

Hum left the store with a lighter mood than when he'd entered but that didn't keep him from miscalculating and sliding the back of his car into a pile of unplowed snow at the end of the parking lot. He tried reverse and forward and made no headway. It wasn't the first time he'd gotten stuck this winter. Before, he'd been on campus and was aided by students who seemed willing to help him as long as he let them make fun of his inexperience, and again at the mall where a nice old man stopped and talked him through the proper technique. Bascomb's was not near other stores. All he had to turn to was Orinda.

He was debating the wisdom of calling AAA and using his own membership card when a thump on his trunk demanded a look in the mirror. A woman in a parka was standing on the pile he was mired in and motioning for him to go ahead, slow. He went too fast and spattered her with snow. She banged on the trunk again. In the mirror he could see her looking at him sideways until he shrugged his apologies.

He tried again, but just kept spinning. Next thing he knew she stood by his window which he quickly opened a few inches. It was snowing only lightly, but he didn't want to invite it into Mason's car. "You're going to have to back up."

"But that will get me more stuck."

She leaned down to window level, cocking her chin to the side, reminding herself that he wasn't used to this. "Listen, who's on First?"

What was she up to? "Um, I don't know."

"No, he's third base. See, if you don't know the routine, you'll screw up the whole bit. It usually works that if you back up, you can maneuver around the ice patch you've created. Let's try it." She smiled at him indulgently throughout the lesson and he finally recognized her as the librarian he'd handed the little girl over to.

She stood out of his way. He watched her while he raised the window, watched how accepting she was of the snow accumulating on her. Smiling to himself with a sense of deserved humility he slowly depressed the gas and backed up into the packed snow he'd just inched out of. He waited while she regained her foothold behind him. Following what he'd learned from the old guy he accelerated slowly then let up for a second to allow the car to slide back some then tried again. Slowly, inches at a time, steering to the side of where he'd gone before as she suggested, he got himself free. When he finally felt some traction he shot ahead, got clear and prepared to go back and thank the woman. He'd learned from before that it would be useless to offer a tip. But when he got out, he found that she lay face down in his tracks. As he trotted over to her she kicked her feet like a kid having a tantrum. He knew from that that she wasn't hurt badly, but her body shook and he thought she might be crying. He came to a stop by her head, unsure of how to proceed.

As she braced herself to rise he heard the laughter. He helped her regain her footing. "I'm sorry, I didn't realize what..." What can you say when you've done something really stupid?

She laughed anew. "What's on Second." Composing herself she shook clumps of snow out of her skirt, stomped her booted feet, threw her hood back and shook her hair out. When she looked back at him, smiling and fresh, she saw that she'd shaken some snow onto him. Removing a mitten she reached up to wipe drops off his face. "I'm fine. But you need some practice." She took his arm and turned him around, started walking him back to his car. "Just do me a favor. Don't drive on the country roads. I don't make it out there very often."

Chapter 12

Cicily Trimble knew that if she was to take credit for this story she had to do some of the information gathering on her own. It had taken her a couple of months to locate and look into the dealings of five on her list. The other two were more elusive. Although she'd found nothing to categorically eliminate the first five, when she got a clue on one of the last two she jumped on it. Her theory was that if they were so hard to find they must be hiding something.

So she was on her way to Brookings, South Dakota to find out about Mason Landers. She'd come upon that location by accident and couldn't be sure that the source was worth believing. She'd finagled someone else into giving her the phone number which wasn't listed anywhere else and found that at least there was someone at the Mason Landers home even if he wasn't interested in new siding.

The drive north on I-29 from Sioux Falls to Brookings is not as bad as Kansas. There are some ups and downs, some long curves. There are interchanges, farmsteads and shelterbelts to break the monotony. But that isn't saying much when there's four feet of snow covering everything, drifts in the median that isolate the lanes and a featureless sky just a shade darker than the ground. There are no towns near the road, no animals, no birds, no bugs, nothing that isn't brown or white. For the next forty-eight miles there are nine things to distract you from your thoughts.

The drive from the airport was a turning point for Cicily Trimble. She had thought that her turning point had come a few days before when she'd gotten a leave of absence from her job, but that was only logistics. That was the process of recognizing that the path she was traveling was like an alley that was too narrow to turn off of. That was the looking ahead for a wider spot and getting permission to go to that wider spot. Arranging the information she already had, getting the news director and the station manager to take the time to sit together, presenting that information to them coherently, that was hard. But that process of saying 'look at me, I'm not just a weather girl' was only getting permission not to be just a weather girl. If she couldn't pull this off, she could still go back and be a weather girl, she'd gotten that assurance. On the drive from the airport Cicily Trimble saw that as long as she had that assurance, she would always be a weather girl no matter how well she pulled this off.

Her dilemma, now that she was close to him, was how to investigate. Was this the guy who was involved in environmental engineering? How does one tell? Do environmental engineers wear certain kinds of work clothes, clean suits maybe? Do they get environmental engineering magazines in the mail? Do they meet with other environmental engineers over coffee at the local Big Boy? Do they have a look, a propensity for clean pen protectors, white sneakers, crew cuts? Is there a fraternity pin, a Future Environmental Engineers of America cap?

And what if he isn't the whistle blower, but a loyal worker, and she alerts him to the fact that there is a whistle blower, is the real whistle blower placed in danger by her ineptitude? Even if he were the one she's looking for, why would he blow his cover by admitting it to her? If she'd already found five on the list and couldn't tell if any of them were the whistle blower, why did she have such high hopes for Mason Landers? Maybe she'd already met the right one and just simply had no idea what she was doing. What were the chances?

Okay, she thought, let's look at this logically. The people who made this assignment to the laptop user believed that the whistle blowing could be attributed to one guy. If so, he'd done his whistling so that his identity had not been divulged. Why? Wouldn't the information be more credible if the whistler's qualification could be verified? But then no one in the industry would trust him; no one who was involved in shady practices at least. So by remaining anonymous he is able to continue working. And continue to whistle again elsewhere. Is he looking for fraud or does he just keep running into it? And is he being paid to come forward or could he possibly be whistling out of the goodness of his heart?

Why would a guy who works on a contract basis make himself so hard to find? If you count on word of mouth for your reputation to spread, don't you want to be accessible to people who've heard of you and want to hire you? And why Podunk? Why isn't he home based in one of the many hotbeds of environmental catastrophe like LA or Hanford, Washington? Do these anomalies make him more or less likely to be the whistler?

Cicily decided about the time she passed the last rest stop not to approach Mason Landers. She would find him, watch him, ask around about him, learn as much as she could about him without arousing his suspicions. Then when she approached him she'd be better able to assess his veracity. Maybe.

Cicily had visited her grandparents in Michigan a lot when growing up. Snow wasn't a menace to her. The wide-open expanses of snow, however, had left her with a feeling of desolation. On her drive up I-29 she had found herself speeding up at times to get there sooner and slowing down as well when apprehension called to her from the empty back seat. When she got to town, even though the piles of snow on the curbs seemed serious threats to safe driving, the mere presence of trees and familiar restaurants restored her sense of purpose. She took only a few minutes to get situated at the Holiday Inn before making her first call to the Chamber of Commerce. She reasoned that they would be able to get her a map of the city and advise her on where certain things could be found. She found that they weren't open and the desk clerk suggested that the library could do the same.

Mason Landers was listed in the phone book and its map told her where it was but not what was around it. For that she knew she needed to see the Polk directory. The library should have that.

Cicily had worn boots; knee-high leather boots with two-inch heels and no fur. They had been fairly good at keeping her feet warm in the car with the heater on full but she hadn't had to walk much in them. The more she walked, the more she wanted to walk faster and the more she tended to slip. She hadn't fallen yet, but she'd come close. She made a mental note to notice what the women she encountered were wearing, because she'd have to get new boots. This decision was reinforced when she walked into the library and saw several people look up at the sound of her heels on the entry floor.

"Excuse me, do you have a Polk Directory?" Jen was the interlibrary loan person and knew the collection fairly well but the name was unfamiliar to her. She shook her head and looked pained.

Cicily sighed heavily and tried again with more sarcasm than she would ever have acknowledged. "It's like a phone book only it lists people by address and phone number."

"Oh, sure, the city directory. I'll get it." Jen went to a nearby bookshelf came back with a paper bound book about a quarter of an inch thick. Cicily, accustomed to four-inch thick volumes for most of the Los Angeles suburbs, was astounded but took it, holding it by a corner as if it were a dead rat. She took it to a table, dug out her notebook and took the map which the librarian had miraculously provided her with and made entries of the addresses surrounding the Landers house. Some of the entries indicated the occupant's occupation, most did not, including the Landers entry.

Before returning the book to the librarian Cicily took a quick look around the library. It seemed to be well used, there was evidence of the availability of the newest technologies, no hay in the corners. The women she saw wore boots, but with thick, flat soles, not the least bit fashionable. She suspected she could buy some locally, but what the hell would she do with them when this story was pinned down?

Cicily decided to drive past the Landers house. It wasn't quite five yet, people would still be at work. She would be less likely to be noticed. She was a little disconcerted to find that the side streets hadn't been plowed as diligently as the main drags, but she made it without crashing into anything. There was nothing special about the house or the neighborhood. They weren't new but they weren't old. They weren't cheap and run down nor were they large nor well landscaped. Modest. A middle class neighborhood.

This revelation disturbed her resolve. She had finally convinced herself that the guy she was looking for would surely have gotten a hefty payment from somebody for spilling his guts. It had niggled at the back of her head all along that it was too weird that a guy who worked with oceans would be living in the middle of the country. She'd come to assume that he must be independently wealthy, or maybe he had family here, something to make it worth the trouble of coming here, which, in Cicily's estimation, was real close to nowhere. And there were no other Landers' in the phone book. This just wasn't panning out as she had expected.

Chapter 13

"Ms White? This is Detective Daniels. You had some more information about the caller?" Bobby, in returning Jodie's call, assumed she had remembered more.

"Which one are you?"

Her abruptness wasn't what he expected. Such an attitude wasn't unusual, many failed to see the value in being polite to the police, but he'd formed the impression upon first meeting Jodie that she was more genteel than normal, enlightened. "Pardon?"

"Are you the one who looks like Dan Akroyd or the one who looks like Festus?"

"Festus? Really? You think Dan looks like Festus Hagen? I've never noticed but now that you mention it..."

Like a juice-filled first grader desperate for an empty stall she hollered, "Which one?!?!" Geez, he thought, this girl is scared.

"Uh, I'm the tall one."

"Fine. Dan Akroyd. Our agency got a call yesterday, which I just found out about because the temp at reception didn't know our clientele roster. Some guy called and asked if anyone here was intercepting calls for Humphrey Dixon. She wasn't sure what he meant by intercepting calls so said she didn't think so and he hung up. She had seen Hum's name on the client list, but the question seemed invasive to her so she wasn't more forthcoming."

"Okay. That's probably good." Bobby was quiet for a few seconds while in thought. "When she answers the phone does she identify the agency? You know, indicate that it represents writers?"

"That's not our practice but who knows with temps. I believe I've heard her say just Beckwith Agency. Although we are primarily a literary agency, that is not part of our name and we do represent other talent."

"Okay. So he won't be sure he got the right agency. We'll be right over to get statements from you and the temp. If he should happen to call back before we get there have her play dumb. Do you think she can do that?"

Jodie took a deep breath. She felt a little more at ease knowing that they found her information compelling. "No. I think she'll have to go with the real thing."

It took Bobby just a couple of seconds to recognize the joke. "Okaay. I'll be right there soon."

Chapter 14

At twenty to eight the next morning Cicily parked her car at one end of the block and sat there watching as people drove off to work. She sat for seven minutes before anyone at all departed. Apparently it didn't take long for people here to get to their jobs. By five after eight she'd noted that the next-door neighbors and two of the three houses across the street had lost someone to the work force and she was frozen to the bone. Although very much wanting to stay until Mason left, she knew she wouldn't last any longer.

She went back to the motel for breakfast and to warm up. While ordering she nonchalantly asked the waitress, "Do you happen to know Mason Landers? I've heard he lives here," but the woman was sorry, she'd never heard the name.

At ten Cicily returned to Mason's street. She drove past his house slowly looking carefully at his driveway. Although it hadn't snowed any the night before she thought she could tell that there were no more tire tracks than there had been when she'd been there earlier. She assumed, therefore, that he hadn't yet left on whatever errands took him out of the house. Cicily pulled around and parked in the same spot. She reasoned that if she didn't walk past his house, Mason was unlikely to notice a strange woman in the neighborhood... if he did indeed know the women in the neighborhood... and if he was looking out the window just as she passed. What were the chances?

It wasn't until she knocked at the fourth of the five houses she'd targeted that she found anyone home. The woman there seemed to be home sick but was willing to let her come in and talk when Cicily proved oblivious to the hint.

"Hi, I'm doing a spot check for the census bureau. Are you acquainted with the man who lives across the street, Mr. Landers?" She had thought this out the night before and prepared a manila folder with some very wordy forms, which she hoped no one would bother to read upside down. They were really part of an application she'd obtained for admission to a country club. She was hoping to take up golf and use the place for exploitable contacts once her career took off. The forms were in a part of her briefcase she forgot to check before heading off. She'd cursed when she'd first found them but now thought it was providence that had left them there.

"No. I've seen him around, but I've never met him. Has he done something wrong?"

"I see. No, not that I know of." Cicily smiled endearingly. "Do you happen to know where he works?"

"No. But he seems to be away for long periods of time. I've always thought that he must work at EROS. We have a friend who used to work there and some of the field workers would travel to foreign countries fairly regularly."

Cicily's brow furrowed. "Air Rose? Where is that?"

"It's down near Dell Rapids. You see the sign on the interstate."

"Ah. Yes. Eeross. I remember now. What is that, exactly?"

The woman looked at her askance. So this is the quality of people our tax dollars pay for. She was very well dressed in a tight black leather skirt and bulky emerald green sweater. The dramatic black wool cape was stunning but didn't look like it could keep her warm, especially in the 30 mile an hour winds common in eastern South Dakota. "It's a facility of the federal government." She nodded pointedly at that as though it would somehow force the census worker to remember, but Cicily nodded and smiled vacantly. Try again. "EROS Data Center. It stands for Earth Resources Observation Systems. They process information from all kinds of satellites. Mostly tracking changes in the world's vegetation. They work with lots of foreign countries." She waited for a sign of recognition but waited in vain.

"I see. And you think he works there but you aren't sure?"

"No. As I said, I've never talked to him."

"Does he have many visitors?"

The woman was beginning to wonder if she was sicker than she felt. "Not that I know of. What does that have to do with the census?"

"Oh, we just want to get a well rounded picture, of the common man, sort of. Would your husband know anything more about Mr. Landers?" Cicily beamed with pride, confident that she was improvising with exceptional ease.

"I don't think so. He would have mentioned something." She decided she'd had enough; she'd have to get rid of this nasty old bear. Perhaps a good sneezing fit would be sufficient to drive this strange person away. Long ago she'd been a featured player in the school's summer repertory group, Prairie Rep. Let's see, a good bout of sneezes should start with a few abortive inhalations leading to a couple of loud shuddering sneezes and a quick reach for the Kleenex. Give it a shot...score!

"Well, I think I'm done here. Thank you for your time. You take care now." Cicily Trimble let herself out with due haste. She nearly slipped going down the steps, grabbing the railing and steadying herself just as she felt the folder starting to slide from beneath her arm. She took shorter steps back to the sidewalk and stood momentarily to collect herself. Maybe one more place. The house on the corner.

The old man who let her in was obviously hard of hearing. The TV blared and he seemed not to notice when she rushed over to turn it down. She guessed it must be 90 degrees inside, which should have been a relief to a beach lover like herself, but she found it hard to breath. She was tempted to shout but found she didn't have any trouble getting him to understand her. No, the old man didn't know the man who lived across the street or anything about him, but he seemed to be gone a lot of the time and since he looked like an intellectual fellow, the oldster thought he must work for EROS. A lot of eggheads work there. Did she know it was a processing station for CIA surveillance? He'd taken the tour and he saw what was behind some of those closed doors.

Great. If he had looked more credible Cicily might have found this to be information worth pursuing, a twist in the plot which might have explained a number of things. But Cicily's instincts told her that this was just a doddering old man of no use to her investigations.

Her luck having run out with the neighbors, Cicily stopped at the records office in the courthouse and found out the assessment of the Landers house and how long the present owner had been there: $74,000 and 4 years. So it wasn't a newly acquired safe house. She found the university library and was disappointed to see that the index of the local paper was not up to date and what there was had no entry for Mason Landers, ever. After lunch (where no one recognized the name, again) she spent some time driving around getting a feel for the place and ended up at the local newspaper office. They wouldn't give her access to the indexing they had available to their own reporters. She wasn't impressed. One could barely call them a newspaper; a few pages justified by the wedding photos and the hog reports. She could have claimed professional courtesy but her credentials failed to acknowledge that eventuality. She even thought of enhancing the minor fall she'd taken getting from her car to the office and using it as leverage. But she was beginning to see that her shoes would get her no sympathy.

She was going back to the motel to call Harlon and have him recheck the data because this guy didn't seem to exist, driving by the Landers house on her way. Just around the corner she slammed on her brakes and killed the engine. There was a car just backing out of the Landers driveway. The car didn't drive off as she'd expected it to. She yelled at him from the safety of her car, "What are you waiting for? Just go around the block if you're lost." Finally it occurred to Cicily that he might have seen her car in his rear view and be wondering if she needed help. Frantically she restarted it and inched ahead. Sure enough, the Landers car drove on and around the next corner.

She was going his direction but a block over. She figured she'd catch sight of him at the cross streets only to find that the grid was unreliable. There were often two or three blocks with no alley or cross street. She was furious until she found a way to get to the street he'd turned onto and discovered that was a safe half block ahead of her. Although she felt confident that she could identify the car she had not a clue as to where he was going so this was her only option. He ended up at the Hy-Vee supermarket. Cicily parked in the next row over which she felt was better strategically but it meant she had to get out to see him, then all she could see was the back of a thick hooded parka.

Once inside Hum slipped the hood back but he knew where he was going and was deep into the store by the time Cicily had slip-stepped her way through the parking lot. It took her five minutes to find him. She checked each aisle three times and was afraid he was on to her and had slipped out the back when she saw the same parka moving from the video rental section toward the milk and beer aisle. There he was, her first good look at Mason Landers. Now she could find him wherever he went.

Chapter 15

Cicily had spent several days paralleling Mason Landers' movements. He'd been to each library several times as well as stops at restaurants and supermarkets. One night she'd just turned onto his street when she saw him driving away. She followed until she saw that he was headed down a street that would take him to the Interstate. Since it was a street on which he would easily be able to tell that he was being followed, she turned off and returned to his place, pulled into his driveway and got out. Cognizant of neighbors who might well be watching she rang the bell then surreptitiously used her heel to make a rut in the packed snow on the driveway, returned to her car and went back to her room.

Things were going more slowly than she'd expected. She'd called Harlon to see if he had more clues for her, something concrete to confront Landers with. There was nothing so she was stuck with prime time TV. She found it somewhat mesmerizing. She decided to catch as many local newscasts as she could and started a file of extensive notes which she labeled Field Research. Who knew what might come of it?

After breakfast she walked by his house, having parked at the corner, and nonchalantly checked his driveway. Her heel mark was unchanged. So, was he running from her, off on a new job or did he have a girlfriend somewhere? This was harder than she thought it would be. If it weren't so cold, she told herself, she could have staked him out and would have known what he was up to. Twenty below was completely unacceptable for any sane human to deal with.

Even were she to stake him out she would not be able to see what he packed in his car before he left. She wouldn't even know what clothes he would have donned. It didn't occur to her that this lack of information severely limited her understanding of his intentions. Nor did she seem to take into account that any strange car parked on the street, whether there was a woman sitting in it or not, would have attracted immediate attention from the locals and a call to the cops who were friends and neighbors, not the faceless, heartless, relentless ticket hounds she had come to think of the LA cops as being.

Without Landers to follow Cicily decided it was her best opportunity to shop. She'd keep checking the drive and if he hadn't returned she could catch the working neighbors in the evening.

She'd gotten some boots the night before at the K-Mart. She particularly didn't want anything she couldn't in all conscience throw away. The clothes were another story. If she found some reasonable things she would likely keep them. There were mall shops that catered to the casual wear of the young and carefree. The phone book didn't list much else. She found a fashionably dressed desk clerk at the motel and was directed to several places which sold clothes as a sideline. These were promising.

Shopping netted her several intriguing pieces. She asked why she didn't see women wearing these kinds of stylish clothes around town. She was assured that these outfits were commonly seen. It wasn't until she'd been convinced that what she really needed was a tougher coat that it dawned on her that coats, utilitarian coats, were what she saw people wearing most. Perhaps under the coats there was evidence of taste after all.

While chatting with the sales clerks and trying her very best not to sound too disdainful of the many things she found lacking in Brookings she made some engaging discoveries. There were acclaimed theatre productions on a periodic basis, one of which she had unfortunately just missed. There was a chamber music group that brought in a variety of internationally known performers, one of which she would be able to see this weekend. The art museum held some world-renowned pieces and an extraordinary textile collection which she went to visit that very afternoon.

This was the best news she'd had since arriving but she wasn't sure if in the long run it made up for the sparse restaurant selections or the lack of a good bakery. It was, however, enough to replace her scheduled date with soap operas and Oprah.

Before she knew it it was time to change into her new clothes and see who was home. Cicily had noticed that there was a factory shift change at four, maybe some of the neighbors would be home then. Only one new face answered a door. He turned out to be a maintenance worker who had a screwy shift so that he could plow snow when the parking lots were empty. He was most gracious to Cicily, offering her coffee and a shawl (needed due to his trying to keep the heating expenses down). He plainly had no one to talk to in his line of work for he took the opportunity to explain to Cicily what a terrible time people had been having this winter. Cicily was irritated at first to be sidetracked but soon found his narrative so interesting that she was tempted to take notes. When he finally ran out of stories about lost drivers being tracked down by their cell phone signals and lost pets being taken in by strangers she asked about Landers and he admitted he knew nothing about him personally. He did, however, know the name of the guy who shoveled his walk and has happy to look up his address as well.

As she was leaving the janitor's house she saw that three other neighbors had just arrived home. One was at the mailbox, one garage door was closing and one was just turning into the drive, no, actually he was being dropped off. Knowing that people hated to be bothered at dinnertime she resolved to get to all three of them as quickly as possible, which worked out well because only one of the three had anything to add.

Mrs. Vacant, who didn't really care what she'd come to the door for, was delighted to talk to Cicily while she prepared her dinner as long as Cicily understood that she couldn't stay to eat. No problem there.

"This is a very interesting neighborhood. Now the man who lives on the corner he had an affair with the woman next door to me while he was home alone supposedly recuperating from a job related accident. It was quite something when his wife found out.

"And the man just around the corner from him, he's a professor. There are rumors that he's supplying drugs to certain favored students. Someone said it was rohipnol but you wouldn't think they'd know about it then, would you? Unless he was like a dealer getting it for guys who then gave it to..." She seemed to realize she was rambling or maybe she just got caught up in the intricacies of lasagna layering.

"Well. Then the woman behind me, we're quite sure she's embezzling from the church fund she is the treasurer of. She bought this brand new Porsche. She's been wanting one for years and we don't know where the money came from. Of course we can't prove that, not like the woman across the street who found out when her child needed surgery that her husband isn't the kid's father. And that's nothing compared to the man on the other corner who's been selling puppies. Turns out his brother has been supplying him from this filthy puppy mill he's been running over in Minnesota for which he was arrested and this guy can't understand what the fuss is about. Can you imagine, seeing all those defenseless animals and not feeling any compassion?"

"No, no I can't. What about Mr. Landers? He's two doors down that way."

"Him. It's rumored that he's got stuff buried in the basement. I know someone who was jogging and saw him come out of his house and dump a bucket of dirt in that flowerbed near the door. Well, I guess you can't see it now, but it's there, trust me."

"What kind of stuff?"

"Who knows? No one saw him bury it. Could be money, could be stolen property, no way of knowing." Cicily couldn't help wondering: maybe a body?

"Well, thank you for your time Mrs. Vacant. You've given me much to consider."

"Are you going to be able to get to the bottom of this stuff? Someone should."

"This stuff?"

"All the goings on."

"You're right, someone should." Cicily made a hasty exit. That left one next-door neighbor that she hadn't talked to but she was beginning to wonder if she should bother.

She decided to call on Mason's snow shoveler. She didn't know how lucky she was to find him at home, but he did. It turned out he had seen Landers only a few times. He was paid for a whole year at a time and had no reason to touch bases with him. He explained that there was no pattern that he had noticed to when Landers was around and that he, the shoveler, didn't pay much attention to when he, Landers, was in town, he just did his job.

Chapter 16

Having lived in Brookings for several weeks Hum had come to feel that he'd successfully blended in. He spent a lot of time at Mason's but went about his shopping and research secure that no one paid any attention to him. People were pleasant and unobtrusive to him as they were to everyone else and he was comfortable being pleasant and undemanding back to them. He'd figured out which stores were the most popular and had chosen to shop when the most people were around. Before a storm, of which there were many, people flocked to the stores and paid no attention whatsoever to who else was shopping in their frenzy to get enough videos, food and batteries to last until the plows came through, allowing Hum to hide in plain sight.

One day in March Humphrey became the subject of discussion at the town's best libraries. At the morning break of the public library staff, when most of the staff took time to gather and chat about what was going on in the library, in their lives, and in the community, Lisa relayed her concern about an incident from the night before.

"That woman was in last night. I've seen her around a lot lately. She's very attractive, dark hair, wears very... tailored clothes. She looks like she's cold." Most everyone at the table acknowledged that description with nods.

"Oh yeah, her."

"I saw her in here in the afternoon."

"I think she's kind of creepy."

"She asked me about this guy who'd just left." Lisa continued.

"Mason Landers?"

Lisa looked at Bryna as if she'd just guessed the color of her unders. "Uh-huh."

"She asked me the other day who he was but I told her our patrons' identities were confidential." Bryna was one of the senior librarians and somewhat of a stickler for the rules.

"Oh... yeah. Well, what she said last night was, 'That guy who just left, wasn't that Mason Landers?' I checked the screen and since she knew his name I thought it was okay to tell her it was him. She said she knew him a long time ago and asked if he came in here a lot. I told her I didn't know since I didn't work the desk all the time.

"So she asks if he's still into the environment, said he used to always get excited about big environmental accidents. Well, how would I know? So I said I could not tell her what kinds of things he took out..." a smug glance toward Bryna to reinforce that she did know and follow the rules, "...and that maybe she could catch up with him if she hurried. But she didn't, she just mumbled something and wandered away. Weird."

"Which guy are we talking about?" Amber, who had been reading the coupon section from the last Sunday paper, was always a little behind, and they found explaining things to her to be tedious in that she usually couldn't relate to what they were talking about once they'd finished.

Bryna took just a second before she spoke. In that time she was thinking: his eyes, which sometimes actually matched the color of his hair, took on the pale brown of sycamore bark; his hair was untrimmed, most likely due to his lack of interest in the impact, for whenever he removed his cap, liberating the curly hair, never had she seen him smooth it down; his features were fine but not feminine, the mouth particularly was small but that only served to emphasize the delight brought to his face by a wide grin. What she said was, "He's about 6 feet, light brown hair getting kind of long, glasses, trim, kind of cute..."

"Kind of!" Linda was shocked by the understatement. In her estimation he was one of the more attractive men to come to the library. However, Linda spent most of her time shelving books and missed out on lots of things; most of which, she was convinced, were more worthy of her attentions than the tasks that kept her from them. She'd seen him a few times sitting quietly at a table or searching the shelves and she was real ticked that she'd never had the opportunity to deal with the new hunk (as she referred to him with friends) personally. It was undoubtedly more tragic for the new hunk to have missed out on dealing with Linda who fancied herself an undiscovered treasure. Of Amber, sitting next to her, she asked, "Have you seen the tush on him? It's righteous."

Bryna ignored the interruption, "...in a quarterback sort of..."

"That's it! I knew he reminded me of someone. Don't you think he looks a lot like Mark Harmon?"

"Jen, don't all ball players look a little like Mark Harmon?" Everyone laughed at this because Louisa had not the faintest idea who Mark Harmon was let alone what most ballplayers looked like. She proudly shunned television and all forms of violence. By their reactions Louisa could tell that she'd been right in assuming that a quarterback was a ballplayer. She smiled as well, but her delight was tethered to the accuracy of her deduction and her perception that the others were glad for her.

The description Bryna spun for Amber's sake continued: "...He wears jeans and sweaters and a big old green down jacket with a Dodgers cap. He seems pleasant enough..."

The whole room could see it coming, a common refrain from Bryna when it came to the uninformed characterization of anyone who seemed nice.   Nearly in unison they filled in the rest, "but so did Ted Bundy!!"

They all laughed and carried on. Serial killers were big draws in the book world and there seemed to be more on Ted Bundy and Charlie Manson than any others. There was no denying his popularity, even after all these years. They laughed, but each knew that she was right. There had been many library users to whom they had attached no particular suspicions who later proved to be unsavory; thieves, rapists, bigamists, molesters. Each revelation had been a disappointment both in the waste of life's potential and in their failure to recognize the evil lurking.

Having given it a little thought Linda said, "I don't think he looks all that much like Mark Harmon."

"More like Mark Harmon that Dick Butkus," Louisa contributed as a joke, and once again, with no basis in understanding, she was right.

"I think what Jen meant, Linda, was that like Mark Harmon he's lean, attractive, he holds himself with confidence like a good ballplayer, used to being watched and appraised by unknown thousands. Actually it's more than that. It's like he spent so much of his life with people watching him that he doesn't even notice anymore. It's just the impression he gives off." Bryna wasn't sure why she was bothering to explain, nor why they were accepting her assessment, after all, Mark Harmon hadn't been a ballplayer for decades. And even as she said it she knew it wasn't right. She'd described the effect accurately enough, of that she was sure and it was sufficient to identify him, but something niggled at her and said the cause was wrong. If the truth had been there, it was now lost.

Linda had reconsidered. "Yeah, I see what you mean. But I think what he's giving off are pheromones. Which is a noticeable change from wet parkas."

The fun was temporarily interrupted to let someone out of a corner to take a phone call. "It does seem that there's something strange going on there. I don't remember seeing him before this winter, not that I see everyone.   And usually when I see her, it's when he's around. She never talks to him, never approaches him, but every time she's talked to staff it's been about him." Bryna usually went about her work purposefully, but she noticed peripheral things in passing.

"What do we really know about him?" asked Lisa.

"I've seen him in during the day a lot, so he must not have a 9 to 5 job."

"Maybe he's an artist, like Andrews. He's always here during the day."

"I don't think so. He's too neat; there are no spots on his clothes or his fingers. And from what I remember of what he took out, it was more like finance stuff. And fiction." Bryna had checked out to him only a few times but there were other times she saw what he brought back. "I almost wish she'd come right out and tell us why she's after him. It would be nice to know if there's anything we should be concerned about for the safety of the staff and patrons." Well, no one could argue with that administrative reasoning, but it sure put a damper on their fun. Good thing break time was up.

While over at the university library a smaller group of staff were just getting down to taking their break. They rarely socialized even at breaks, but now and then Janice would bring a cake or chips and dip just to get them together. All of them had had occasion to notice the woman who had spontaneously become the topic of discussion. She'd caught their attention on her day of arrival when she walked down the hall clacking in her high heels, like a summer bored kid running a stick along a fence. No one in their right mind was wearing anything but waffle soled boots this winter.

Geri worked part of the day shift in circulation. But as a student, she was unauthorized to answer any of the questions posed by the woman the only time she approached the check out desk. Since Geri had seen Janice, who worked mostly in reference, talking to the woman for some time one day, Geri asked her, "What does she want? She never checks anything out, she always seems to be just sneaking around. Is she FBI or something?"

"No, if she were from some police agency she'd have to identify herself as such. I think. She pointed out this guy who was sitting over by the windows and asked if I could tell her what kinds of materials he'd been requesting. I told her no," Janice continued with a sly grin, "he hadn't requested any materials. Strictly speaking he'd asked for information not materials and it was none of her business what he was looking for.

"He has been quite pleasant every time I've dealt with him; respectful, he's listened carefully and patiently. He even came back to thank me for steering him in the right direction. She, on the other hand was demanding, manipulative, disdainful. You know the type. Always expecting someone else to be doing the digging." Yes, they all knew the type. When it involves class work, finding the information is as much of the learning process as what is found, so most librarians are leery of those who demand.

If someone had asked what Janice liked about this guy she would have pointed to his physique, his quiet manner, his intelligence, because Janice had never acknowledged the two things that most of her loves had had in common; strong hands and eyes that were just a little closer together than most. She watched people's hands when she talked to them, tried to find a chance to touch them.

Over the years there had been some delectable men that she had passed by because their hands had repulsed her by being too fat or too long. This guy would not know that fate.

"She's been doing this for several days and each day she's hung around for over an hour just wandering." Kate, whose job quite often was to go around and pick up the materials that people had left on the tables, was in the best position to watch the goings-on. "Every couple of minutes she'd glance around a corner to see if the guy was still there. Then she'd make like she was looking for something on a shelf, maybe pull something out and open it for a while. God, she was making me tired just watching her waste time!

"He's kind of fun to watch, really. He'll be reading something and then kind of lower his head sideways. He'll leave his elbow on the table and run his hand through his hair as a cover for what he was doing which was trying to watch the woman without appearing to."

"Sounds like that's exactly what he looks like he's doing."

"Yeah. He's clearly not very good at it. 'Course, she's not much better at watching him. After awhile he'd get up and leave and she'd mosey over to see what he'd been looking at. Once," she laughed thinking about it, "he picked the aisle she was in as his route through the stacks. I was working at the far end of it and saw that she kind of shuddered like Wile E. Coyote when he runs into a wall. It was like she really wanted to make a run for it but didn't have time, so she buried her nose in the nearest book. I had to move my cart two aisles down so she wouldn't hear me laughing."

"Did he say anything to her?" asked Janice.

"He looked right at her as he passed by but then went on his way as though she was no one special. She must have been real disappointed."

"So, what kinds of things is he reading?" Geri was intrigued.

Kate had made a point of picking up his stuff before anyone else added to the pile. Given the woman's actions she'd almost been tempted to make some kind of record of the items in case there was something fishy going on, but when she saw that they were so tame she decided not to. "Oh, estate planning, foundations, some South Dakota regulations, the codified laws."

Janice concurred. "Yes, that's about right. He had me help him track down some stuff on setting up a charitable foundation. Rather obscure, almost to the point of being things you might expect to have to go to an attorney for, but he seemed to follow it without difficulty."

"I've seen him looking at microfilm, the Argus Leader for the last few years." They were all looking at Clarie expectantly. "That's all. I've only seen the woman once, but I could tell right off that she was watching him. He had his back to her so I don't think he knew." Clarie was exceptionally quiet. If there'd been somewhere else to drink her coffee she probably wouldn't associate with the rest of the staff at all. She'd perfected the art of being seen and not heard to the point of being almost invisible. Every once in awhile she spoke up. Something in her hoped that these occasions were of great insight and that the people to whom she chose to speak would find in her words the key to the secrets they wrestled with. They had yet to muster the wisdom to do so.

"Do you think he knows she's following him? He seems to just go on about his business. You'd think that if he knew, he'd be trying to avoid her." Geri read mysteries of which the university library had few. The prospect of a real life mystery in her midst was most appealing. The others nodded or shook their heads in silence. "Why do you suppose she's following him? She doesn't strike me as the lovesick sort."

Kate was quick to reply, apparently having given the matter some thought already. "No, I suspect it's something more sinister than that. Maybe his wife is trying to get the goods on him. You know, a philandering husband."

"I don't think so, he doesn't have a ring."

"I agree. I saw him at the play the other night and he was alone. Seemed to be having a good time. He talked with the people around him, quite friendly." Janice had felt quite self-satisfied at having gotten his eye. It was clear to her that he'd been intrigued.

"Maybe he has mob connections and she was sent to kill him." Geri had hopes for a bigger scandal developing.

"Oh yeah, that's it." Janice was becoming fatigued by their groundless speculation.

"Say," beamed Kate, "did you hear about Francis? He was caught peeing on cars after the bars closed last Wednesday. Very hush hush." Yuck.

Chapter 17

Things were pretty dead when the phone rang. Hardly anyone was ever around to listen in anyway. "Yeah?"

"So what did you find out?"

Harlon recognized the voice right off, and he wasn't glad to hear it. "Why didn't you just call the studio yourself, Evvy?"

"Because I'm not as smart about these things as you are." Not as smart at some things, Evans thought smugly, that was true, like with computers, but he sure knew enough not to expose himself to scrutiny. He hadn't gotten this far by doing obviously stupid things. He knew that the studio would check their caller ID. A call from a TV station would be considered legitimate and their questions more likely to be answered. His deadpan delivery was sufficient to convey the real message.

"Yeah, I forgot. The writer has an agent with the Beckwith Agency in Santa Monica. Her name is Jodie White. Number's in the book."

"Fine. That should be enough for a while. If I need more, I'll be in touch."

"Yeah, I'll be here waiting," Harlon smiled at being equally adept at irony.

Chapter 18

The shoveler, who actually used a snowblower for most of his work, got to thinking after Cicily left that her questions didn't really jive with her story about checking out service possibilities for her aging mother who was to be cared for at home. He mentioned his discomfort to his friends at breakfast the next morning. Most of them were street people, men who used to or still did work in the street department, on street construction or grounds maintenance. Some of them had already heard about a woman who was asking a lot of questions around town. Just as he was about to leave he saw Cicily waiting to be seated and pointed her out to his friends.

There was no conspiracy involved. It had not been his intention nor his directive that his friends make any effort to deceive her, it just turned out to be the most logical thing for each of them to do. As luck would have it, this was the day Cicily had planned to visit a number of restaurants and ask the customers about Mason Landers, since she had found the servers and hosts had been completely ignorant. She was delighted to find that there were so many who had something to tell her. Small things maybe, but they all would work together to form a whole picture, one that would help her nail Mason Landers. Why the hell, she asked herself, hadn't she tried this before? She gathered half a dozen statements, each with a little something else to follow up on.

With this and the stuff she's picked up from Mrs. Vacant Cicily finally felt like she had some investigating to do. And just when she was beginning to find this place interesting.

Chapter 19

Snow, to a California desert kid, was a delight and a mystery. Hum's family had vacationed in the mountains from time to time, he wasn't a greenhorn at snow, but he was still an apprentice. He'd checked out Hoeg's *Smilla's Sense of Snow* from the library, but, though it was a good book, it was about Greenland snow, ice flows, glaciers, tracking bears. All he could relate to was the crunch of tread-upon snow, the wet versus dry snow, the windblown snow.

He'd noted the various weights of outdoor apparel in the closet. He'd discovered that shoveling in a heavy coat left him too hot, that it wasn't always necessary to button up, that the scarf worked better inside the coat and what gloves were better for than mittens.

He'd established some rules about shoveling the snow. For one thing, it was taking longer to shovel the same amount because the piles had grown so high. Either you couldn't heft the heavy snow high enough to reach the top or what you did get to the top slid right back down to your feet. He could no longer shovel blindly. Each scoop had now become an addition to a sculpture. Sometime he would shove the top of the pile off to leave more room, sometimes he'd strategically place the boulders thrown up by the city plow near the top to create a barrier which would keep the loose snow from falling back down and sometimes he gave up and walked to beyond the high section to where the scoops could be easily dumped. Sometimes, when the snow was wet, it stuck to the shovel and you had to whack it against something hard to get it off. Whacking it against the top of the pile only started avalanches and revealed to Humphrey why it was that Mason had multiple mittens, gloves, caps, and jackets.

Also significant was when to shovel. Sometimes if you shoveled early the sun would melt the last layer and your concrete would be dry. Sometimes it would just freeze it over and make a very nice ice sheet. Sometimes if a lot of snow was coming it helped to shovel during the storm to cut the depth in half, but other times the wind would fill in what you'd shoveled and you'd have just as much as if you hadn't bothered.

Driving in snow was a skill he was proud to have mastered. He'd learned by watching how to barrel through the ridges temporarily left by the snowplow. He'd learned how to turn the corner so that the fishtail skid brought you all the way around. He'd learned how to see just enough of the road to make it back home through a ten inch square of unfrosted windshield. He'd learned which intersection gutters to come at on an angle and which streets were only half as wide because the plow couldn't get to the curb.

He was walking to the university library one day when up ahead he saw someone slip on an icy patch and let fly all the things she was carrying in order to keep from falling. He realized, as he got closer, that it was one of the librarians. He would have stopped to help regardless.

"Oh. Hi," she said as she surveyed the debris around her. "I'm on my way to a meeting and I wanted to look professional so I didn't wear my heavy boots. At least I didn't break anything."

The wind was stronger where they stood than it was out in the open due to a funnel affect. He felt the force at his back and decided on the best course of action. "Why don't you stand there and let me hand you things. What goes in the box?" He crouched down and placed back in the box the things that had been dislodged. The other things he handed to her then picked up the box and stood. "Perhaps you should hold onto me."

"By the way, I'm still looking for that piece that you wanted to see. Is there a rush?"

"No, not at all."

"Well, if I can't find it here we can interlibrary loan it."

"But I'm not a student."

"Ah, well, you can take what I find and have the public library get it. Whoa!" A gust had caught her again and blown her hat off.

They went on to her car before Hum returned to retrieve the hat. Along the way he chatted, "I was talking to this old guy at a restaurant one day. He said that the most useful invention was the motor vehicle turn signal. At the time I thought he was probably a little loopy, I just nodded and let it drop. Thinking of all the inventions that seemed like a pretty paltry one to champion. But a winter like this, the number of times there was whiteout on the highway, the piles at the intersections so high you can't see around them, I tell you, without that little blinking red light I'd have been in half a dozen accidents just myself."

"That was probably Finnias. Darrel Finnias. He's quite a character. Professor emeritus for the engineering department. Holds a couple dozen patents of his own.

"Thanks for your help. I'll let you know next time you're in what I find."

"Like I said, no rush."

Chapter 20

"Jodie. What news do you have for me?"

"Nothing." She'd squabbled with herself on and off for several days now about telling Humphrey that Horace Evans was getting closer. The fact that she'd been able to put it off seemed to be the significant factor in the deliberation. There had been two calls since she'd had the cops over which they felt might have been from him but in both cases he'd been vague and noncommittal and the numbers he'd called from had been pay phones. She needed to check in with Hum about his work so she consciously put her next move in the hands of fate.

"You aren't at home are you? I hear wind."

"I'm on my way back from Sioux Falls."

"Aha! Been to see the nice woman who likes jazz."

"Yeah." His tone was not that of a man returning from a rendezvous. Hum was not given to one-word answers. There was much left unsaid here. Why was Hum being hesitant? False modesty at his age?

"What's the matter Hum?"

Humphrey quickly checked his surroundings. The weather was crappy. He knew it was already snowing where he was headed but the traffic was light and he knew what to expect from this stretch of the interstate. The cruise was on, no coffee to absently spill on himself. He felt protected. He saw himself safely strapped into a fighter cockpit, ejector control close at hand. "Jodie, now don't get upset, but I think someone might be following me."

"What!!!" He quickly pulled the phone away from his ear. Jodie wasn't given to speaking loudly under any circumstances. He'd scared her and now he regretted it.

"Maybe it's nothing. There's this woman. I didn't see her around town when I first got here and all of the sudden I see her everywhere I go. It's not like she's behind me when I walk down the street, but she just seems to be wherever I end up."

"But you said it was a small town, there aren't that many places to be."

"Jodie, this isn't a one horse town, there are a hundred places to go. It's highly unlikely that someone else would have the same agenda I do.

"Anyway, I decided to go down to Sioux Falls to see Pam and check to see if anyone was following me on the interstate. It looked clear and we had a good time and all but when I asked Pam if I could stay for a few days she wanted to know why. I should have planned a cover story from the start and fed that to her when I came down, like I was having work done on the house or something, but I wasn't thinking. So I told her about wanting to avoid this woman who was following me and she went ballistic. She wouldn't believe that it wasn't some girl from my past that I was trying to avoid because I'd done her wrong. She called me names that I don't think applied," he was most indignant about this, "and threw me out. So I'm on my way back."

"Well, Duh! Hum, you write such wonderful women's parts. When are you going to apply that understanding to your own life? And just maybe it's time to get out of Dodge."

He knew she didn't mean that. It would mean a delay in his work. Also, where would he go? Short of jabbing a finger on the map and holing up in a rented room he had no one else to go to, no options. "I don't want to move again. If they're really onto me, leaving will seem to them like I'm confirming their suspicions.

"First thing I have to do is verify that this chick is following me. Then find out why. Yeah, there could be lots of reasons. She could be after my body." Humphrey remembered some of the places he'd noticed the woman and imagined her reaching for him when he wasn't looking, flexing her fingers in longing for his firm buns and licking her lips as though he were the best chocolate on the menu.

"Yeah, right! New woman in town and her best bet is Humphrey Dixon?"

"Hey! May I remind you that you don't know what you're missing?" Right then Jodie decided not to tell him about the calls. It could wait for further developments.

"I have a small idea of what I'm missing and I emphasize small. But you're right. It could be anything. Could be nothing, especially if she's after your body.

"Hey!"

"Hey, since your jazz lady threw you out, maybe you should give this woman a chance."

"No way. I do the picking. Besides, I have other possibles in mind."

"Like who?" The flurries had been negligible but as soon as he hit the county line the snow started coming down thicker. Being as cold as it was the flakes blew off whatever they landed on and he didn't need to turn on the wipers.

"There's this librarian at the college who seemed very interested in making me happy. Not overly attentive, (you know how I hate it when they faun) but she put a lot of time into helping me find some things."

"Hum, you know they all want to make you happy, even the hags. I'm assuming this one isn't."

"She's very charming."

"Un huh."

"She has great legs. She reminds me of Arnold's wife with the dark hair, the jaw, the pointed nose, bright, inquisitive eyes. I saw her at a play and she wore this skin tight T-shirt. At work she wears these tailored suits in blues and grays which are flattering but not especially appealing. I guess librarians have a code, huh? I got the feeling that if I'd sent the right signals she'd have helped me with all kinds of stuff." This last being said with a lecherous growl.

Jodie had heard Hum wax eloquent about the virtues of nearly every woman he met. Humphrey laudably found worthwhile things in everyone. According to him it just happened that they fit so well into his characters. "Like your story? Maybe she can be the star. How's it going?"

"Story's coming along fine and she wouldn't fit. First draft is about a third done."

"Great. I got the pitch and I have no complaints. You might want to think about introducing your con man earlier and maybe having a love interest for him to disappoint."

Humphrey felt comforted by this bit of advice. It meant their working pattern was re-establishing itself. "Yeah, I'll look into it. Gotta go now, off ramp's coming up and they can be tricky with snow pack and one hand on the wheel."

Chapter 21

Hum was beginning to feel at home at Bascomb's. The sound of the door opening brought to mind a candy shop he'd frequented on his way home from grade school. Although he avoided familiarity in most of his dealings, here he didn't feel it posed a danger. He'd gotten a couple more bouquets for non-existent ladies. The workers would just nod when they saw him come in because most of the time he just wandered around and the only times he had spoken it was with Orinda.

Based on Jodie's harping he was fighting hard his inclination to use Orinda as a model, she fit so perfectly what he had envisioned when he'd come upon the idea. There was a natural predilection to pattern characters after real people. Didn't they always teach you to go with what you knew? It was imperative from a legal standpoint that what was used was not so on target that it constituted liable. But Humphrey usually felt that since he'd come up with the idea of the character before he'd thought of who that character was like, that he was safe, ethically.

With Orinda, whom he liked immensely, he felt it would be a disservice to make her a movie character. He needed to be sure in his mind that there was something delightful about Orinda that he did not, could not, incorporate into his shop owner. He couldn't remember a time before when he'd found a suitable character within a suitable site and this also gave him pause. When he found the perfect diner to match his concept, the waitresses actually working there seemed bland. He'd found the perfect car salesman at the dentist's and the perfect teacher at a second hand store. His brother had never figured out he'd been the model for a psychopathic killer and that's exactly how Humphrey wanted it

When he would walk into Bascomb's what he mainly noticed was the lack of things. No one rushed to dog his every step. There was no soothing music, no coffee to bribe him, no neon, no specials. And most significantly to Humphrey, no screaming scents; no incense, no scented candles, no air fresheners. It smelled of flowers, of damp earth, of "fresh". Just like you'd expect.

Orinda came out from the back with a new arrangement. She proceeded quickly past Humphrey and placed it in the window display. He had cocked his head to one side, sizing up the affect, when she turned toward him.

"Well, how did your arrangement work out?"

Humphrey was momentarily stumped. Oh yeah, he'd asked her to make up something meaning scout. She'd come up with a kind of grass for facilitator and fennel for strength. It was bland so she'd thrown in some roses. She'd said they were multifloras and it meant grace. "Fine." He'd taken it home and smiled for Jodie whenever he passed by it. "Can we try another one?"

"Of course. This is part of the fun for me, knowing the hidden meanings behind the arrangements. Usually people ask for the flowers without knowing what statement their mingling makes." She looked again at the placement in the window, went back to make a slight correction, and returned to her front counter.

"This is for somebody who is very smart, very resourceful, someone interested in preserving safety and providing justice."

"Ooo. I can do some of that, but not all. Very smart is something called Venice Sumac. I don't have that, but I have something close. Just plain smart might be considered walnut. I don't know of anything that represents resourcefulness, maybe dogwood, it's used for duration, of course it's not available right now. Justice is rudbeckia, you'll recognize that. But safety, I don't get much call for that either, it's called traveler's joy. There's juniper which means protection, maybe I could work that in."

"Are you remembering all of these meanings?"

"Yes. I make notes when I get back to the car. There was the one I kept for myself, 'pity the poor sods who endure this winter', that was pine and lettuce and chamomile and gilder rose."

"Guelder."

"Guelder. Then the ivy for fidelity, mint for virtue, bluebell for constancy and those wonderful burgundy roses for unconscious beauty. I'm going to use that one again. It smelled as good as it looked."

While she worked Orinda ventured a query. "Mind if I ask you something?"

Humphrey stared at Orinda for five seconds. Why did he have a bad feeling about this? He considered Orinda a good person, safe for him to associate with. Although she'd readily told him many personal things, she'd never asked him more than was necessary for the business they conducted. Finally she looked up at him and he felt compelled to answer. "Uh, sure. What is it?"

"There was a young woman in here a couple of times. A rather conflicted woman, way out of her element. She was asking about you." Orinda went about her business, not watching Humphrey at all. He had not considered that Orinda would be contacted. His failure to anticipate that disturbed him. He felt the wall closing in. He saw himself telling an investigating detective "It got darker, I swear it did." Why had he assumed that his connection with this woman would not be seen and exploited? He didn't remember visiting Bascomb's since the woman had started following him, but maybe she'd started before he was aware of her. He suddenly felt guilty just being there exposing Orinda to the sordid aspects of his deception.

"Ah. I think I know who you mean...at least I think maybe it's someone I've seen around town. But I've never seen her before. I don't know why she's asking about me."

"It didn't sound to me like she knew you. How do you want me to deal with her next time?"

"You think she'll come back?"

"Undoubtedly. She knew you'd been here often and didn't believe me when I told her I knew nothing about you." Orinda finished her arranging and presented Humphrey with a lovely bouquet.

"But you do know nothing about me. Surely there's no need for a strategy." Humphrey was fumbling for his cash and didn't see her raised eyebrows. "I'm sorry she's bothered you, Orinda. I truly don't know who she is or what she wants." He smiled, but it was strained and incomplete. "If I could keep her away, I would. Thanks... for the flowers." He turned abruptly and left. Orinda shook her head in disappointment. He had purposely not told her anything about himself, it wasn't just shyness. What had he gotten himself into?

Chapter 22

"You know, I don't think that woman has been in lately." Geri was bringing to Janice some papers that had been left at the front desk. She welcomed the chance to talk to someone different and check out the action in reference.

"What woman?" Janice had been concentrating on the progress of an Internet search she'd been doing for a professor. He'd looked for the information himself but couldn't find what he thought ought to be there so he'd asked the librarians to verify that he needed to go to extraordinary means. It was a boring task, but thoroughness was a matter of pride for Janice who was determined to elevate the respect afforded her profession. Others in the department had been delighted to leave the task to her.

"The one who was following that guy." Geri absently fingered the other papers on the desk, oblivious to any questions of confidentiality.

Janice looked up momentarily to scan her internal database. "Oh yeah. You're right, I haven't seen her lately. Has he been in?" There were thousands of students enrolled, although only a fraction saw the benefit of using the library resources for research or documentation in writing papers. The hundreds of faculty and staff, oddly, seemed to match the ratio of non-use. Even so there were only a few dozen who requested her services repeatedly, she tended not to keep track of the rest of the users. And of course she didn't work all of the time or even spend all of her work time at the desk.

"Yeah. I saw him this morning." Geri had noticed earlier that Kate was preoccupied in her usual duties, lingering in one area longer than it looked like was necessary. She'd casually investigated and found the object of her interest.

"Did we find out any more about them, why she's following him?" Janice knew that if anyone were going to pursue the puzzle it would be Geri. Even if others gathered the information it would be Geri who would compile it.

"No, not that I've heard."

"Do we know names for either of them?"

Geri brightened at that reminder of her newest discovery. "Oh, I was talking to Jen, from the public library, I wondered if they had been there too and they have. She said they were just as curious about them as we are. They're wondering if there's something fishy going on. She said that the guy checks things out there. His name is Mason Landers."

"Really! Hm." Janice raised both eyebrows and her attention was definitely shifted from the search to the newly processed information.

"What?"

"Nothing. It might be useful to have a name. And interesting for a librarian to have divulged it. I wonder what Bryna would have to say about that. Did you look him up?"

Geri jerked to attention. Why would Janice assume that she would go to the trouble of looking up his name in the other library's files? In her effrontery she was hesitant in responding. "Yeah, he only has their card." She decided to ignore the remark about Bryna. It was well known that Janice considered Bryna a lightweight, not up to her professional standards. Geri didn't want to get between the two of them.

"That fits. He doesn't really seem to be doing research for course work."

"How can you tell?"

She turned to look at Geri indulgently and replied with sarcasm. "Has Kate mentioned seeing him looking at abstracts or theses? It seems he's just looking things up, not laying groundwork. The real question is who is he?"

Hadn't she just told her? Was Janice beginning to lose it? In Geri's estimation it was only a matter of time. She couldn't pass up this opportunity for condescension and a cocky head tilt. "He's Mason Landers. He has a regular local address and he got the card years ago. He's used the card recently and has no history of fines." Janice was amused to find that Geri had researched the matter that extensively.

"So, he's been a good boy. Well, that answers all our questions then doesn't it?" It most certainly did not, but Janice returned to her searching and Geri, having used up her welcome, returned to her post.

Chapter 23

Cicily had spent considerable time following up the leads she'd gotten from the people in restaurants. The momentum she'd thought was finally building was turning out to be a momentary spurt. Refusing to recognize it as such, she decided to reward herself with a break in the action so she could sit down and organize her research. Many of the notes she'd taken were on scraps instead of in her notebook, which she often found to be an inappropriate recording tool at the time she received some tidbit. She spread out all of the notes she had on the bed and read them over a couple of times looking for patterns, similarities, themes. Cicily expected this task to be exhilarating, the documentation of her gut feeling. She expected it to be a task that flowed, that cleansed. She had no anxiety about this task, she'd put it off purposely so that she could relish it, like the sweetest part of the watermelon left to eat last. Poor Cicily.

If all of these people were to be believed, Mason Landers regularly spent time in three places simultaneously, was a member of three major families and was very effectively duplicitous. He may be kind of cute, but it was hard to believe that so many diverse people would accept so many obvious lies from him, in a place like this where the truth would eventually come out. There were so many conflicts in the various accounts she'd gathered over the last week that she was amazed that the locals, as stupid as they obviously were, had not seen it themselves. How could it be, she railed alone in her motel room, that she hadn't seen these conflicts as they mounted up? Sure, she'd realized that there were discrepancies, but that was to be expected, wasn't it? She couldn't be expected to remember every little detail while in the midst of an interview wherein she was passing herself off as someone who cared.

She threw herself into the chair by the little table, her limbs sprawling haphazardly like a doll no one cared about. Her inclination was to go back to the notes, to study them again, to try to figure out who of those she talked to could be trusted to help her ferret out the truth. But on what basis would she make that decision? Her gut certainly hadn't served her well so far.

When Cicily finally made the decision to call Harlon it turned out to be too early. If she called him at work the call would be logged. Unable to stand looking at her useless notes any longer she went to the bar and started a series of whiskey sours. Well past dinnertime, she returned to her room bouncing lightly off the walls of the motel hallway. The call went through immediately. "Harlon, sweetie, have you got any news for me?"

"Sweetie? Cicily are you all right?" He paused and before Cicily could answer he asked in a whisper, "Are you being held hostage or something?"

Cicily pulled the receiver from her ear and looked at it wondering how she'd picked up some cop show on this little walkie-talkie. "No, of course not."

"Seems to me you would call someone Sweetie only if there was a gun being held to your head."

"Now, Harlon, where did you get that impression of me? Of all things. Now you just put that thought out of your head. You need to tell me what you've learned about our quest."

"I'm getting nowhere with the other leads. It's possible that your laptopper is deleting leads as he gets to them."

"He can do that?"

"I don't know about him, but it can be done. I have found you some new information about your clues. Some other companies with whistleblower problems."

"Are any of our suspects related to these companies? What about Landers?"

"There's no clear picture. Involvement is spread out across the board."

"Well give me the names related to Landers. There's definitely something wrong with the situation here."

"Cic, why don't you just confront the guy?"

"Don't call me Cic. Never. I'm no one's sister. I won't stand for it."

He could hear the dull thud of a foot being stomped on the carpet. "I hear people call you that all the time, but fine, for you, no Cic. Now, why not talk to the guy?"

"The time isn't right yet. I'm hoping to get more information from the locals that I can use."

"Sure you aren't a teensy bit afraid of him?"

A sharp intake of breath betrayed her. "Don't be asinine. I'm not afraid of anything. I'm just taking my time to develop the whole picture. Get a feel for the environment. People don't just flutter down from trees, they are reflections of where they grew up. I've never lived in a small town. I need to get a feel for this place, the pace, the priorities, the ... Why am I telling all you this? Your job is to provide me with the leads, not evaluate my methods. I'll move when I'm ready. I have to trust my instincts.

"Now, give me those names."

Chapter 24

There weren't many people in the library, one of those unpredictable lulls. Humphrey stood at the counter and waited for the librarian to look up from the computer she was frowning at. She was the one he'd dealt with the most. He'd been impressed by her confident disposition, her competence and she'd made him laugh. He liked her look as well. Trim though not particularly athletic, short auburn hair, a mass of loose curls (curlier than his own) accentuating her thin neck. Big, round glasses with moss green frames were the only ornament he'd seen around her face in contrast to the large bangle bracelets she wore over the cuffs of her sweaters. Being a little taller than average aided the look of the somewhat out of date soft paisley skirt and boots that she wore, good quality classic designs which transcended fashion trends.

Noticing her looks was a welcome distraction. He'd thought all afternoon about his next move. This was getting bigger than he'd first thought and he needed information to better evaluate it, so he'd come to his librarian. He envisioned her in a spotlight dressed in a sparkly royal blue tatter dress singing "Simply the Best" with a trio of gray haired librarians behind.

Amidst the trouble she was having, eventually the librarian remembered to check on what she was neglecting, having vaguely taken note that someone was near. She smiled in embarrassment when she saw who it was.

"Do you need some help?"

Most librarians, like other public service people, develop a set of phrases that they have found to be most reliable. For Bryna her opening inquiry was designed to be concise and unobtrusive. Actually she'd discovered the phrase long ago when her cat responded to it. Whether it was the cadence of the words, the inflection in her voice or the combination of consonants, she never figured out. Oddly enough it hadn't worked with her husband, but then, not much had. She only asked it of people who showed signs of confusion, impatience, or abandonment. She wanted least of all to be like a hovering store clerk or a librarian at her college of whom she would not have asked for help unless her life depended on it. The woman had treated her like a potential shoplifter, asking to help her every single time she walked up to the card catalog. Every single time the woman assumed Bryna knew nothing, had learned nothing, would never learn anything. It was enough to drive Bryna to be the kind of librarian she would have liked to have had around. She thought of the woman often and that thought acted as a subliminal trigger for Bryna to curb her natural enthusiasm. She thought she'd gotten her public face down fairly well, too. As she saw it it was inviting without being promising, confident without being snotty, open rather than eager and smiling without being demonic. A delicate balance did librarians maintain and yet her colleagues insisted they could not act. She knew better.

He smiled at her and blinked. He leaned close over the counter and spoke quietly. "Hi. Me again. I don't want to impose on you greatly but I was wondering, have you noticed a woman around lately who seems to be following me? I know that sounds paranoid."

It struck her as it hadn't when she'd described him earlier that his whole demeanor when he spoke to her was different from when he was off working on his own. When she saw him in the stacks, huddled over something on a table or dropping things as he tended to do, he reminded her not so much of Mark Harmon but of someone not fluent with the local language or culture. He was isolated, oblivious. Whereas when he dealt with the librarians he was quite charming. His charm, the smile, the steady gaze, the attentive stance, was like a translator, an interactive mode, used only when needed. "Actually, I have seen her."

"Oh, OH! Well...is she here now?"

"I didn't see her come in and I haven't noticed her lurking." Lurking, he thought, yes, that's what she does. They stared at each other for several seconds. "Maybe she's waiting outside." He turned to face the door, she looked that way too. In unison they shifted to look out of the windows on the opposite side. It was getting late but with the cloud cover and snow flurries one could still see well enough to tell if someone was sitting in a car or standing around. All that either of them saw was a woman coming in with three kids and a guy walking a dog. They stared at each other again. He nodded. She smiled at him broadly. 'Yes,' she had determined, 'this guy needs some help.' She started walking toward the door into the staff area. "Why don't you come with me?" He gave a little start like a dozer who's just been awakened by the slightest of noises, and followed. She pointed to where he could sit. "I have to stay out here for a while longer, why don't you just relax?" He sat hesitantly but after she'd returned to the desk he leaned back and closed his eyes. He tried to put himself in a peaceful place by thinking of rain, the glorious rain falling softly on his face after one of the many droughts he'd been through as a kid.

Ten minutes later Bryna returned somewhat breathless. "I was filling in for someone's break. How can we help? Do you know who she is, what she wants?"

Hum shook his head dejectedly. "I don't know. I was hoping you could help me figure that out."

She looked incredulous. "You don't know who she is? But you knew she was following you."

"How could I help but know? She shows up everywhere I go. I never see her coming in but when I turn to leave, there she is. It's getting creepy. I know this is a small town, but people don't keep going to the same places day after day."

"You do." He looked at her, astonished, as though she'd ripped open the entire family's Christmas presents. "You come here, you go to the campus library, you go to Bascomb's, to Southtown, to Sound Station in the mall and you go to the Dairy Bar, sometimes several times a day..." Hum found himself trying to gasp, in shock at finding that he had been noticed. He suspended listening. "...which isn't so outrageous really. I mean I would love to have the time to get their ice cream for break. Well, maybe in the summer."

When he saw that it was his turn to speak the effort was more than he expected. At first it was coming out as a whisper, he struggled to reach normalcy. "How, uh, how do you know that?"

"I've seen you, people who work at those places have seen you. Like you said, it's a small town and people don't have murders to talk about."

Murders? Hum was beginning to think he'd made a mistake by saying anything. If everyone in town knew of his comings and goings, they'd probably told the woman. He imagined people with binoculars and walkie-talkies stationed in every store on Main Street. Thus warned of his progress the people in the store he walked into would have time to hide their scouting tools. No wonder he hadn't noticed anything!

"See, you didn't used to go that often, so one could surmise that you were going to these places so often now in an effort to verify that this woman is indeed following you." She used her hand to illustrate the progress of her argument. "Her name, by the way, is Cicily Trimble. Ring a bell?"

"Vaguely," he mumbled not really aware that he'd spoken aloud. "How do you know her name?"

"Credit cards. She's charged a few things around town. She needed some warmer clothes. A friend of ours owns the best dress shop in town. Cicily asked our friend about you so our friend thought it only fair that she ask about Cicily. It's a little game we play at bridge." Hum envisioned a room full of Mrs. Cleaver types sitting in fours at card tables while the librarian dressed in fatigues stood before a chalk board labeled "Target of the week", marking key sites on a crude map of downtown.

"What else do you know about her?" he asked falteringly. She knew that he was unsettled by what she said. She sensed that he was closing in on himself, struggling to process unexpected information while presenting a blank if not calm facade. She ached to reach out and reassure him, to touch him, to run her fingers through the hair which had not been cut since his arrival and was starting to form ringlets. But she'd learned to suppress that familiar urge. If he hadn't been so self absorbed he'd have seen all this in her eyes, and then, for the briefest moment, he might have seen a shift in the angle of the eyebrows bringing the eyes open wider: predator quickly restrained.

"Not much. There's speculation that she's from LA. She's been here about a week. She asks everyone about you and seems to tell everyone a different story about why she's asking. No idea what she wants?"

"Huh? No. No, I don't know what she wants. Uh, what is she doing while she's watching me, what kinds of things does she ask about?" It was a stalling question. Hum was figuring that the smartest thing might be to just cut and run, get out of town before this went any further. Geez, the whole town knew about him. This was not hiding.

"She keeps busy. It's not like she just stands and stares at you. And her questions vary. I know she asked one of our staff if you were still interested in the environment. And I think a couple people mentioned something about a connection with the sea and accidents." Hum winced involuntarily. "There's not much consistency to go by. She hints at a secret about you that she's privy to." Hum noticed that the other people working the night shift were glancing in as they passed the door, becoming more curious about the man and what was going on.

"Listen, I've taken up enough of your time." He rose to leave.

"But you still need help." Bryna had done so well at not responding to his discomfort that Hum found himself wondering if she was trying to hold him there until either that woman or the cops showed up. Even if he was wrong and she was sincere, could he really trust her?

"Possibly, but I don't think there's anything you can do. Thanks."

Bryna moved so that he would not feel trapped. "As you wish."

Chapter 25

"Jodie? I need your help with something." 'Til two in the morning Humphrey had wrestled with how best to proceed. He tried talking it out to himself, a technique that often worked with script problems where he needed to relate to the lack of ethical dilemmas of psycho killers or the strain of being a state park security guard, but he wasn't able to place himself in a different perspective here. He rarely called her at home, he knew Jodie would still be up and he hated burdening her with the news of further troubles, but he had no one else to turn to.

"Fine, we'll trade."

"Why? What's wrong?" He knew it. He knew the guy would get closer.

Jodie'd had some time to think about it and her initial panic due to the resurfacing of Horace Evans had completely disappeared. She told herself that her reasons for proceeding had an order of priority. She told herself that helping to remove the danger posed to her friend Humphrey was the most important factor. She told herself that helping the cops was the wisest, safest, most civic-minded thing for her to do. She told herself that preserving the life, talent and storyline of her potentially most lucrative client was merely a lucky perk in the deal. She didn't mention to herself that by playing a part in the resolution she put herself in line for co-author royalties. Herself had considered earnestly and replied with a resounding, "Do it!"

"We think this Evans guy called the agency..."

"Shit!"

"...a few days ago. Those cops came by right away when I called them about it. The agency has caller ID so we were able to get a record of where he called from, but it was another pay phone. The cops are in the process of setting it up so that they can lure him in."

"Jodie, don't do it, it isn't worth it. Remember this guy is already wanted for murder." He envisioned hovering about ten feet over a guy resembling a black and white Paul Muni, walking the streets in black and white prison stripes, black gun in hand, drums throbbing on the background track, technicolor people passing him completely oblivious to the danger he posed. "I'm not placing you in danger. I'm coming back now."

"Humphrey Ulysses Dixon, you'll do nothing of the kind."

"I'll confront him myself before I let you be bait."

"So you'll be bait instead?"

"It's me that he's after." Why was there any question that this was the right thing to happen? He should have been more forceful with the police. He should have stayed in LA and drawn the Fool out a long time ago. He could have found people to help him trap and catch the guy. If he went back now he could rectify that error.

"Exactly. He won't harm anyone who can lead him to you. If you were actually here, then he would have no use for me. I'm not taking this lightly, I know he isn't benign as we once thought, but Bobby and Dan assure me it will be okay. He may not bite anyway. I'm not going to argue with you about it Hum. What is it that you need?"

"I thought they were going to set up a trap for him at the answering service. It wasn't supposed to get as far as your number. How did he manage to get ahold of that anyway?" Hum might be able to laugh in the face of possible danger but putting Jodie at risk was not something he was willing to be responsible for.

"That's just it, it wasn't my number; it was the agency's number. It doesn't look like he bothered with the answering service. Dan told me that they'd talked to the staff and setup their trap but no one came, no one called back. Even if he got there a long time ago and coerced something out of one of the employees, that wouldn't explain how it is that he got the agency number since the answering service had my number. He must have found some listing of writers and their agents. Who knows? Maybe someone at a studio told him.

"But forget about that, what do you need?"

"Will you stop changing the subject? I'm not that easily led astray. What exactly are you going to do and when is it going to happen?"

"Well, there's a really interesting clue these guys figured out while I was talking to them. They were thinking about when best to set it up because it seems to be such a long interval between the times that this guy tries to get in touch with you. So, Dan gets this bright idea and has someone check and it turns out that each of the tries (for those we pinned down) has been on a Tuesday or a Friday. They think it must have something to do with when he has time off. After all, he is trying to maintain an alternate identity. So they figured Friday.

"What they're going to do is wire my office and phone. Then they're going to set their stuff up in a spare room and wait. If he calls we'll have the receptionist put him through and I'll try to get him to come in to see me. If he comes in, I'll try to get him to talk and incriminate himself so that they can get it on tape and storm in before he has a chance to do any harm."

"Jodie." She sounded so enthused. Why wasn't she seeing the dozen ways it could go wrong?

Jodie didn't want to argue with him or upset him unnecessarily. "Maybe you're right. You know, they said that they could use a policewoman. I'll call them and have them change the plan. Now, for the last time, what do you need?"

She waited while he decided to give up. "I decided to talk to this librarian." That sounded more daring than it was. He remembered being seven and having to ask the librarian to help him find something on Pitcairn Island. It was the same librarian he'd had to deal with when he'd lost a book and had to pay for it. He thought she would hate him for having been irresponsible. It took all the courage he could muster and a push from his father, not so patiently waiting to drive him home, to approach her. He'd been so apprehensive he didn't notice at first that she'd been quite willing to help him. His dad had teased him on the way home. 'Librarians are just people. They're not the mob or nuns with some kind of moral vendetta.' So he naturally thought of them as machine gun toting, cigar smoking, black habited sisters. Until he got to college and dated one for a semester. No, they weren't nuns.

"The one at the college who had possibilities?"

"No, this one is at the public library. It turns out that everyone's been noticing that this woman that I thought was following me is really following me." He flashed again on the sight of shopkeepers with binoculars and walkie-talkies. He changed the angle of the shot to rooftop looking down. The wider angle clearly showed Cicily shadowing his every move as well as dozens of well-equipped people crowding the rooftops, the leafless trees not impeding their view. Himself crossed the street at one of the midblock crosswalks, turned to the north to see God directing traffic from the church at the end of the street and he finally noticed the change as the watchers pulled back from the roof edges and those in doorways reverted to normal behavior. "It's the lead story in town gossip. They found out her name is Cicily Trimble and they think she's from LA. She's asked them about me but they haven't told her anything. At least the one I talked to hadn't."

"Hum, they don't know anything about you."

"That's what I thought, but apparently that hasn't stopped them, maybe it's even encouraged them. The whole town's buzzing about how she's following me."

"And the librarian told you all this." Jodie didn't see why he should confide in this person.

"Yeah. I figured if you can't trust a librarian who can you trust? Also I saw this Trimble woman talking to her one day. Since she wasn't checking anything out I wondered if it was about me. Turns out it was."

"You know Hum, I think that might be the name of one of the local weather girls. I can call around and find out."

"Weather girl!?! What the hell would a weather girl be following me for?" He tested in his mind the possibility of weather girl as a cover for hired killer. Knife hidden in an umbrella? Ligature as part of a scarf? Gun tucked into an ample brassier? But weren't killers supposed to blend in? Wouldn't this be a bad moonlighting choice for someone seen on TV every day? Ah, of course, LA, home of grade school classes on makeup. His picture turned into a cartoon where Cicily's face pulled off intact to reveal Gabby Hayes.

"Maybe you were right and she's after your bod."

"If she were just after my bod she would have talked to me, not the librarian."

Jodie couldn't argue with that. Something occurred to her. "Hum, you've assumed she has some connection with Horace Evans but maybe she isn't after you. Maybe she thinks you're Mason just like everyone else in town does."

"Hey, that could be. They said she was asking something about accidents and the sea. I thought that cinched the connection but it really wouldn't be my lead question if I was looking for me." He envisioned a Sgt. Friday notebook being flipped open to show a list of identifying clues. Glasses? Talks to himself? Dodgers fan? Disarmingly handsome?

"I don't suppose this has anything to do with the librarian looking like oh, say, Julia Roberts?"

"No. What difference would it make what librarians look like? It's what they know that's important." He stopped and fingered the remains of the last two flower arrangements he'd gotten, found the wilted blossoms and pulled them out. So much for constancy and virtue.

"So she's a hag?"

"No. Actually she's buttonfaced. Kind of reminds me of you." It wasn't that Bryna looked anything like Jodie, she was taller, lighter colored hair not so curly, her eyes were a pale blue instead of brown, but she seemed to be able to see right through him the way Jodie did. She knew nothing about him, what she thought she knew were things she knew about Mason, but she still made judgments that were right.

"I am not buttonfaced," Jodie said with as much dignity as she could muster considering that she had noticed just that morning that she was just as adorable as she was ten years ago. "Did you ask the librarian if the woman asked about you by name?"

Hum knew she would change the subject. When she was working Jodie made absolutely no consideration for how cute she was. "No. And that's a good point. I should do that."

"Then what?"

"What do you mean?" Sometimes late at night, like now, when there was a cloud cover and no street noises, no TV on, no computer fan, no furnace, no refrigerator running, the train whistle sounded like it was coming right at him and he thrilled with anticipation. People often called it mournful, Hum could never see why as if his logic was unrelated to that of the rest of the world.

"What if you find out this woman isn't looking for you but for Mason? You just gonna tell her she's got the wrong guy?"

"No. I guess I couldn't. I can't expose Mase. I don't know what he's been up to, but... If this woman thinks Mase is here, if she came here looking for him... What if letting them know I'm not him and he isn't here puts him in danger? What if my not being him and knowing they're looking for him makes me expendable?"

"Hum, isn't that a little melodramatic? I mean if you don't even know what he does, how can you assume that there's any danger?"

"Because I don't know what he does. If it were ordinary, don't you think he would have told me?"

"Maybe it's just something he's ashamed of."

He thought. Could it be? World travel, unused wealth? Could it be drugs, white slavery, arms dealer, new site trainer for McDonalds? The CIA was more believable. Safer for Humphrey to believe. Who could he trust? Where else could he go to hide? "No, I'm sure he's happy with his life."

"So what are you going to do now?"

"Just get some sleep, I hope. Thanks Jodie, you've been very helpful. Good night."

Chapter 26

Janice seldom put her work aside to dwell on personal matters. She rarely had time to do so. But this was a matter that her mind seemed intent on dealing with. She was trying to read some reviews in a journal but realized she'd gotten to the next page and didn't know what she'd just read. This guy wasn't who he said he was, of that she was quite certain. But where was the other guy? And why was this guy so confident in his impersonation? He'd been here for weeks, apparently unconcerned that the other guy would show up and expose him.

Janice watched as the woman moved from aisle to aisle testing for the best viewpoint. She awkwardly held a bulky coat in the crook of her arm while handling one of the large volumes that were all that was available in that section. With quick and disgusted movements she abandoned what was obviously her best viewing prospect and moved over to where the books were easier to manage. In this less burdened position she started fidgeting with her clothes.

Janice didn't remember seeing her in this getup before. She must have had to buy some new clothes and found them beneath her usual standards. Janice decided to let her fidget for a while reasoning that she'd be more open to distraction after a period of irritation. Five minutes later she approached with a printout in hand.

"Can I help you find something?" Janice smiled broadly as the woman put the book back on the shelf as quickly as she could manage only to find that it was upside down. Janice passed her to the end of the aisle and made a show of peeking around to see the man sitting near the window. "Oh, him again." She paused to relish the look of guilt and embarrassment that passed over the woman's face. She'd obviously thought she had gotten good at hiding her subterfuge.

"Tell me, why are you following this guy?" Cicily stared at her, transfixed, then turned to leave just before Janice caught her arm. "No, really, I'm not just being nosy. He spends a lot of time here. If he's dangerous I think we have a right to know about it." The woman considered this and in turn took Janice by the arm and pulled her down the aisle to where she could still see him but not be heard.

Janice immediately pegged her as a non-user. Anyone who'd studied in a library knew that noises carry in the most unpredictable patterns.

Cicily opened with, "Do you know him?" Janice considered. There might be advantages to letting Cicily blurt out her secrets. But the guy might still be able to hear them so she decided to keep the advantage to herself, a softer whisper was in order.

"No. He's never had to identify himself." Cicily nodded, accepting that she would get no help from this one. Still, she was dying to talk to someone.

"He's Mason Landers. He lives here but is gone much of the time. I have reason to believe he's responsible for blowing the whistle on some alleged EPA violations by several companies. I'm having trouble putting together any corroborating evidence."

"I see. And in what capacity are you seeking evidence?"

Cicily hesitated, one eyebrow arched. Why should this hick need to know the truth? "I'm a reporter."

"Ah. And you've talked to people who might know?"

"I've talked to lots of people. Most of them don't know anything and the rest have been lied to."

"Why don't you just ask him?" Janice gestured toward the man just when he was gathering things and reaching for his coat, giving the women time to move out of his way like hostages tied to the same impediment.

"Because...because I need corroborating evidence." Geez, Cicily thought, this woman is dim. "If I ask him he'll just deny it. I need testimony from other people."

"People who you say have lied to you?" Janice was having a good deal of fun with this.

"People..." could it be that they were the ones who had lied? "...people with no stake in the case."

"Maybe, if he's really a whistleblower like you think he is, he would welcome the publicity."

Cicily gave her a little scrunch faced smile. Why was she wasting her time with this person? "I don't think so. If he wanted to be known he'd have come forward."

"I see," Janice nodded, eyebrows raised to convey the enlightenment she was supposed to have just received, "you're assuming that he's probably broken in somewhere to get the information he's used. You think he's operating anonymously because there's some duplicity involved." Just for a second Cicily's face froze and Janice knew she hadn't considered that at all.

Masking her internal confusion Cicily replied indulgently, "No. I think he just...

wants to continue his work. Thanks for your help." She walked away, got five steps and realized that she still held a book. She returned, gave it to Janice as if she were another piece of the matching furniture, and walked away muttering. Janice felt sure she heard "insufferable" and congratulated herself for a job well done.

As soon as Janice had taken her seat again Geri was by her side. "Sooo, what did she say?"

"Not much. She doesn't think he's a criminal. She actually thinks he's been performing a public service but she's reluctant to confront him."

"Maybe she's afraid to blow his cover... assuming he has a cover."

"Please! By following him everywhere she's made him as conspicuous as a Daktronic sign. I have a feeling this will all blow over soon enough." It was just a matter of picking a time.

Chapter 27

Hum got up later than usual, but he was no longer distressed by the dilemma. He had business to take care of. Shoveling.

Although shoveling had lost its appeal several weeks before, his first chore was to take the shovel out to the sidewalk. It didn't need shoveling but he used it to even out the corners at the gutter. How useful this one pile of snow was becoming. The cause of a good aerobic workout on a somewhat regular basis, the source of countless minutes of soothing inspiration, the subject of several rolls of film and now a quite believable cover for checking the streets for a red rental car. He stood in the cold smiling like a 16 year old with a new license. When a neighbor came out to go to work, he waved.

Hum had a plan. By the time he got to the library it was open. Plenty of time to double around and make sure he wasn't followed. He figured the Trimble woman knew his car when she saw it, but knowing she wasn't close helped in the calculation of his timing.

"Excuse me, there was a librarian here last night. I don't know her name. She has big glasses." He may have thought of her as attractive, but referring to her as such might seem to imply that the others were not.

"Sure, that's Bryna. She's here, I'll get her." The friendly, gray haired librarian went into the back room passing the tall, gray haired, rather serious librarian who was on her way out. Humphrey looked up to catch the short, dark haired, friendly librarian looking back to her work after having watched him. She had noted that he was wearing running shoes instead of boots and that his coat was unfastened. It was in the high 20s outside, things would start thawing today. People were eager to discard the vestiges of winter. He'd removed his Dodger's cap as he'd walked in and was absently fluffing away hat hair as he waited.

"Hi. I'm glad you came back. You were a little upset when you left." Bryna appeared to be genuinely happy to see him again. That intrigued him.

"Can we talk somewhere? I don't want to intrude on what you have to do, but I need to ask you something else." If he was going to use her, he better not be annoying.

"Sure, you need information, don't you? That's what we do here. We'll sit over here at my desk. It's kind of out of the way, but there's this weird funnel affect that lets you hear just about everything. If you listen carefully you can hear who's coming." Before moving away from the counter she looked askance at the short, friendly, dark haired librarian who nodded pleasantly.

"Bryna," Hum said as they walked, "that's an interesting name."

"It means protector. My mother was a romantic."

"And you're not?"

She looked up at him with a tilt of her head. "I didn't say that. She grew up in the hippie era. She's very into..."she paused to find the right word, "...symbols."

Humphrey got right down to it. "You talked to Cecely Tremble. I was wondering if you happened to remember what exactly she asked." There were two chairs near her desk in close proximity. She often thought, when entering her area, of a sculpture which had come to her campus on tour and was so beloved by the students that they bought it: Sandy in Confined Space. Sandy being nude was an immaterial disparity between their situations. In this confined space Bryna chose the chair usually used by the 5 year olds who visited her.

"It's Cicily Trimble, 'I's not 'E's. At least that's what the credit card said. First she asked who you were, then she asked someone here to confirm that you were Mason Landers..." Hum's blood thumped loudly in his ears but he continued to nod reassuringly. Quite involuntarily he smiled. He knew better than to retract the smile because it would undoubtedly be misinterpreted. He'd learned this from a former girlfriend who was generally assumed to be a happy, always-friendly person. More often than not, Hum had discovered after five humorless weeks, she was just squinting. "...said she thought she'd known you a long time ago. She tried several ways to find out what kinds of things you were interested in, but, of course, we wouldn't tell her that." Humphrey looked at her questioningly. She wasn't even looking at him but seemed to know what he wondered. "Federal privacy laws." Ah, he mouthed. "She seems to have used a number of different stories around town to explain why she's been asking about you. You know," she leaned back and spoke offhandedly, "you would think if she was an experienced investigator she would have constructed a plausible cover beforehand so that she wouldn't be likely to trip up." Bryna looked straight at Hum and smiled. He smiled back and nodded without really understanding. She recognized it as an I'll-go-along-with-this-cause-I-don't-want-to-look-dumb grin. She'd seen them often.

"It seems, however, that some of the people she's been talking to have decided to teach her a little lesson in honesty. I know of one who told her you spent most of your evenings at Ray's Corner."

"That's a bar downtown, isn't it?"

"Uh-huh. It's a smoky cave where all the good old boys meet and decide the path of the moon. The guy assumed she would park herself down there and try to blend in. Perhaps she did." Hum pictured the polished, well-coifed, overdressed woman sitting quietly at a standard bar table. The noise filters in, the scene pulls back to show a dozen men in jeans and seed caps, in cowboy boots, in sneakers, in overalls and plaid shirts sitting at tables and at the bar staring at Cicily Trimble and mumbling to one another.

"There were apparently a couple of people who told her you worked at EROS because she tried to confirm that and used it as part of her story." Hum chose to neither confirm nor deny. Bryna noted that and went on. "Of course no one that I know of told her you didn't work there. That would have been too easy.

"Some guy told her you were the illegitimate son of a former city official. You don't see many of them in here so you can imagine what caliber of intelligent creature we're talking about. This guy pointed out that he wasn't disparaging you. He thought of it as a double negative kind of making a positive."

Hum smiled at the librarian, a little unsure as to whether she was reporting accurately or making this up along the way. "Well, that's really thoughtful of him. But why would these people be lying to her about me?"

"My guess is they do it because they know she'll believe them. She comes around telling her own lies expecting that everyone is so dumb they'll accept everything she says and spill their guts. There's a kind of justice to it, don't you think?"

"But they don't know me, why not just give me up?" Hum's hand reflexively reached up to knock himself in the forehead but he covered by running his fingers through his hair. When he recovered his senses he found the librarian staring at him, her head tilted to the side, a grin on her face that said Aha! you know someone's after you! He was forced to shake his head in sheer amusement at his own stupidity. Good thing he wrote scripts because he sure couldn't act in them. "You know, I've taken up too much of your time, again..." She reached out as he rose and touched his hand. He stopped and watched her as she quickly stood from her nearly crouched position, leaving them standing very near.

"No. Wait. Really. We'd kind of like to know how you want her handled." She backed out of her area, increasing the space between them, but he followed step until she could turn and walk beside him.

"Handled? Like UPS versus Parcel Post? Ha ha. I'd like her to go away. Not like send her to the cornfield, Anthony, just for her to go back where she came from. But she probably won't take a hint."

"No, she doesn't seem the type, does she?"

"No. I'm thinking the best thing would be to just ignore her. She probably has a life somewhere that she'll need to get back to before too long." They strolled toward the front door, Hum twirling his cap between his hands, Bryna focusing peripherally on those who might be watching.

"Don't we all. So you think that if she is led to believe you are just an ordinary guy, she'll go away."

"I am an ordinary guy. I know nothing of interest to her."

"You know, to his librarian, Stephen King is just an ordinary guy. It's all a matter of relativity." Bryna could hear her staff speaking her name and turned to see them making the phone sign. She put her hand on his shoulder and pointedly looked him in the eye. "I'm glad we were able to talk again. I'll let some people know how to proceed with Cicily and we'll see what happens." In seconds she was out of sight. Humphrey forgot that he'd intended to look up a couple of things and left the library. He'd also forgotten to look around for the woman and was opening his door before it occurred to him. He took this as a good sign.

Chapter 28

"Bobby, isn't it? Now that you've got clearance for everything, I'm sure this won't make any difference. I know I told you to go ahead with the policewoman but I've decided that you can't go with a stranger substituting for anyone here."

"Ms White..."

"Our business must be allowed to proceed without interruption. If it doesn't, someone's sure to blow the cover. It might be different if we had a limited clientele. If just a few people came in, it would be easier to pull off, but there will be dozens of people in during the time you're likely to set this up and these are not people who will let something slide. They are very observant, very curious, very challenging. That's what makes them good writers and artists. They will make a fuss about anything that isn't as it should be, a loud fuss. I'm sorry, but that's just the way it has to be."

"I've just come from a talk with your boss," he pointed upward, "and he seemed to think it would work out fine with a policewoman."

"That old geezer," Jodie's boss was a mere five years older than she but he was so tight in his outlook, Jodie had come to believe that he was raised by hippies and resolved to denounce all of their carefree traits. "He doesn't see how things are handled on a daily basis. He's probably thinking about liability, not about the success of the operation, which is what concerns me. It's my client who is the focus here, you're just going to have to do it my way, that's all there is to it."

Bobby had to smile. He'd dealt with people in the entertainment industry before and somehow they'd never measured up to their projected image of altruism. Whether they were the victims, perpetrators or relatives of such, their main concern was controlling the publicity. Few of them would have stuck their necks out as this one seemed intent on doing. "All right. We can deal with that. We'll have to look around, make further assessments. We'll have to show his picture to the staff." The intercom became alive long enough to inform Jodie that her appointment had arrived.

"Sure, sure. Go ahead. But..." Dan and Bobby had turned to leave, not wanting to detain her further from her business. As if in song and dance unison they looked back to attend to what she had to add. "... what if he's already contacted someone and gained their loyalty? Wouldn't that just tip him off?"

"Yes, that's true, but just the fact that he called favors the theory that he hasn't had time to make any contacts here yet. And if he has, they've already figured out who we are, haven't they? We'll apprise them of the gravity of the matter and the danger they would face if they cooperated with him." Jodie stood as they turned to leave.

With the door open Dan turned to call out to her, "And you will check into a deal for the foreign rights, that's a dear." Bobby gave him a sharp whack on his arm and Jodie had to hide her smile from the young woman just coming in.

Chapter 29

"Jodie, I'm so glad you're still alive." Despite his flip delivery it was of unusual importance at this time for Humphrey to hear a familiar voice.

"Huh? Oh, nothing's happened in that matter yet," Jodie said impatiently, "so what did you find out?" Hm, thought Hum, so much for my concern about her safety.

"You were right, Cicily Trimble is looking for Mase."

"And she is a weather girl," Jodie added with a note of triumph. Humphrey envisioned Jodie before a studio audience of clapping people and a three-camera setup saying, "and what do we have for our winners today, Bob?"

Humphrey shook his head. "Jodie, that just doesn't make sense."

"Apparently she has aspirations of reporterhood. She's taken a leave of absence to pursue some story. That's what my inside sources indicated. Officially she's on vacation." Jodie's inside sources usually specialized in deals and percentages. Who knew she also had her thumb on local station personnel?

"Mase's story?"

"He must be part of it. Any ideas?" All Jodie knew about Mason Landers was Brookings and that he had once roomed with Humphrey. When he'd set up this retreat she'd respected his need for secrecy. Like the Santa Monica cops she'd viewed the calls as a nuisance only and had encouraged Humphrey to leave only to get him working again. She was confident that she could keep Horace Evans away from Hum but if something about Mason was threatening Humphrey it was beyond her control and, apparently, his.

"Not a clue and I'm not about to jeopardize whatever it is he's hiding."

"Hum, are you even sure he's hiding something? Maybe he's independently wealthy and just off enjoying himself."

He sorted through the junk mail that had piled up. "No, I can't see that he wouldn't tell me if that were the case." He tried reminding himself that not all secret occupations were dangerous. Chemists in perfume factories go through security checks. He knew of realtors who worked for celebrities but never let on so that the deals wouldn't be inflated. People who scouted out production locations always have a bogus cover story. And would you really want your neighbors to know you were an IRS auditor?

"Before you said he was happy, now you insist he's hiding. Maybe he's ashamed."

He would be if he were IRS. "He's an engineer. How much could an engineer have to hide?"

"Let's see. Drugs, illegal aliens, high tech weapons, computer security codes, porn ring, counterfeit gems, hired killer, stealth technology,..."

"Okay, okay. You forgot the CIA and the Energizer Bunny. I don't believe any of that. There has to be another reason and I'm not sure I even want to know what it is. If I can just get the Trimble woman to lose interest and return to LA."

"Maybe you should introduce her to Tracy, then she could get tips on losing interest." Ouch! A bit caustic for Jodie. Regardless, Humphrey found himself envisioning a meeting on Rodeo Drive between Tracy and Cicily Trimble, two lovely chums in shades and flowing dark curls, bored to death with Humphrey Dixon and moving on to raving on each other's purchases and sharing skin care tips.

"I don't see any other course possible. I think the people in town will help discourage her. If she's not really a reporter..." something sounded familiar there, "...she'll probably just give up."

"That's your plan?" she asked incredulously. As a scenario it lacked finesse, not up to Humphrey's standards. With a shake of the head Jodie reminded herself that this was real life, not a plot that could be manipulated.

"I always go with simple when I can, Jodie. Plenty of time to elaborate later."

Chapter 30

Cicily had had enough.

Once she'd decided to confront Landers she had to figure out where to stage this important event. If she went to his house he need only close the door on her, or, worse yet, fail to answer. A public place. In fact just about any of his usual haunts would do except the library, since there might be yelling.

Humphrey felt a cold coming on. Not finding the red rental anywhere he felt safe proceeding with his errands. At the very least he needed something to help him get to sleep at night despite the aches and sniffles. A quick stop at the drug store seemed eminently reasonable. He'd read the labels carefully, chosen the night time cold medicine and was just on his way back to the checkout wondering if there wasn't something he'd forgotten when Cicily Trimble came around the corner and collided with him, resplendent in a red wool suit. As he stepped back he realized that she had a microphone in her hand (although she was holding it about waist high) and was coming toward him again.

"Mr. Landers, I'd like to ask you some questions."

Humphrey found that he didn't have to feign astonishment. Sure, he'd expected, nay hoped for, her to show up, but here? "What?"

"Cicily Trimble, Mr. Landers, I have reason to believe you were involved in leaking information about the McGinty water pollution case and the Hartsung contamination AND in the prevention of Baker Oil getting off-shore drilling licenses in three communities in Newfoundland." Humphrey backed away from her and scrunched his face as if she were a month old carton of milk begging to be smelled. "Isn't it true Mr. Landers that your personal agenda is to expose cases of environmental pollution which have been carefully covered up by the perpetrators?"

"I... excuse me, I don't know what you are talking about. Who are you?"

Cicily dropped her microphone hand and leaned in to whisper conspiratorially.

It was with considerable personal satisfaction that she said, "I'm a reporter Mr. Landers and I am looking for a whistleblower. I believe you are that whistleblower and I want to help you get your story out."

"I don't have a story. You have me confused with someone else." Humphrey could see that there were people watching them. There weren't many in the store, but they all seemed to have chosen this time to head toward his aisle. He decided it would help his case with the locals if he appeared to be harassed and infirm, so when he raised his voice it had a definite stuffed up tone to it. "Now please (cough), leave me alone."

"Mr. Landers, I happen to know you have worked with a number of water based companies and that some of those companies ran into trouble with the EPA after you left. I know about Hancock, Batelle, Rosey Wong Tow and Crenshaw Waxler." Cicily was triumphant in demeanor. She'd taken the offensive, she'd gotten all the names right, she'd demanded recognition. How could she lose?

Humphrey looked around at the people watching, raising his hands in bewilderment and despair, the cold products he grasped only added to the impression of powerlessness. Cicily, spurred on by her audience, mistaking their attention for support, stepped closer. "I know about these entities. I know there are people looking for you, people who want to stop you, people who won't let you continue in your crusade. You're only chance is to go public. Let me put you on nationwide TV and there's no way they'll have the balls to persecute you. I, Mr. Landers, am your only hope."

Hum looked around at the faces waiting for his reply. Straightening his back and swallowing with exaggerated and non-existent discomfort he took a deep breath and spoke quietly but clearly. "You are neither Obiwan Kenobi nor a thing with feathers. I don't know you, I don't know what you are talking about and I do not need your help. Please, just leave me alone." Humphrey started to shoulder past her but she blocked his path. He leaned back and looked her over from head to toe before turning to appeal to the crowd.

Although they didn't know him well they remembered seeing him throughout the long hard winter. All they knew of the woman was that she was new and had made a nuisance of herself all around town. That was enough for a chunky little woman dressed in a pink snowmobile suit whose gray hair bristled from beneath a red and black stocking cap. She stepped up and grabbed Humphrey by the elbow and dragged him around to the next aisle. When Cicily followed and made noises of protestation, not even whole words, the woman turned abruptly and spoke to her nose to nose in a loud whisper. "You got no claims on this boy. Leave him be." Cicily, feeling she'd just encountered a New World version of the evil eye, stood her ground but let the woman take Humphrey up the aisle to the checkout joined by others of similar intent.

Humphrey, caught firmly in the grip of an impromptu vigilante squad, grabbed a quick glance over his shoulder at Cicily and saw the rear guard, hands on hips, following her as she turned and regally headed for the door. Those who carried him along, confident in the efficiency of those behind them, didn't bother to look back but took him straight to the counter, relieved him of his cold products and asked if there was anything else he needed; tissues, soda, juice, ice cream is good when your throat is sore, fruit. Had he needed more they would have dispatched couriers to obtain his every wish but he insisted that what he had in hand was sufficient. Looking down on the bevy of protectors still alert to a counterattack, he had to smile at their courage, initiative and instincts. He wondered, oddly, if any of them packed a gun.

Not until later did Cicily think that she might have learned something if she'd asked the store patrons what they knew about Landers. She remained oblivious to the obvious, they would not have talked to her.

Chapter 31

What with all the sympathy from the women at the drug store, Humphrey was feeling rather good about the way he'd handled Cicily Trimble. He wanted to tell someone about it and there were only two choices so he stopped at the library to see if Bryna was working. There were those things he'd forgotten to look up anyway. He saw himself in a fine Italian suit, dashing dress coat draped around his shoulders, confident smirk transforming his face, the seasoned provocateur checking in with the field commander about another job masterfully completed.

He didn't want to have to ask for her again. Such a step might be noticed by the staff and start unnecessary rumors. One of the staff had already noted his arrival and turned to the phone. When Bryna didn't come out right away he thought he must have misinterpreted what he saw. He picked up the latest Wall Street Journal and sat at the nearest table. He'd been there for some time, becoming unexpectedly engrossed in an article, and failed to notice the arrival of a different librarian.

Janice looked out of place in the public library. Her clothes, consisting of ironed jeans, cowboy boots and a fur coat, were more formal than necessary on a day off. Her shoulder length hair curled under just enough, a feat worthy of a $200 stylist, which took Janice an hour and a half each morning. From a distance the carefully applied makeup diminished the prominence of her sharp jaw line. In grade school she'd been a natural choice to play the witch at Halloween and did so gratefully at first, but the request had come far too often for it not to have had some affect. Janice was generally thought of as attractive but upon closer inspection it was more an impression of her style than the quality of her features. Her imperfect face was one reason she tried so hard to keep fit.

She picked her spot, pulled out a book at random (it was a large print edition of Asimov's Foundation) and feigned studying it. As soon as she caught sight of Bryna she pulled out a cell phone and dialed.

Bryna had been in the stacks retrieving an item which she took back to the phone. She read something out of the book to the caller and looked around while listening. It was then that she noticed that the needy man had returned and seemed to be trying to catch her eye.

She had to answer a couple of more things before she could get away to speak with him. A twinge of guilt made her look back to be sure that she wasn't leaving the others with too many patrons. That matter dispelled, she headed right for him.

He stood and leaned over the newspaper as though to show her something he wished to discuss. "I didn't expect to see you today."

"The weirdest thing just happened."

"What? The sun came out?" She didn't bother to look at the window. Want of sun was a common malady among patrons all winter.

"No. I went to the drugstore for some cold medicine and Cicily Trimble came after me. She was waving this little microphone in my face and asked about these places M..." oops, almost said Mason. Almost forgot that he hadn't confided completely. "...she thought I'd worked. She was accusing me of exposing the apparently illegal practices of a bunch of companies."

"So that's why she's been following you."

"Yeah, but the weird part was that when I tried to get away from her and she got louder all these women, other shoppers, crowded around and they defended me. They drove her off."

"Who were they?"

"I don't know. I don't think I've even seen any of them. Total strangers. Why would they come to my defense?"

"Why not?" He was about to take his coat off when he saw Bryna look over his shoulder. Her smile showed concern.

Janice had seen the cop car drive into the parking lot and had sauntered back toward the door to catch him before he had a chance to inquire at the front desk. She whispered to him and pointed with a nod of her head rather than her fingers. She wanted the maximum surprise factor she could arrange.

As the cop clanked his way toward the newspapers Janice skittered through the children's area and positioned herself where she could watch the confrontation.

"Excuse me," began the policemen. Fred was known to Bryna by sight. He'd responded to calls many times but otherwise she'd had no dealings with him.

"I'm looking for Mason Landers." She looked at Humphrey with a smile, expecting him to speak up. She was still being the helpful librarian not yet appreciative of the implications. "Can I see some ID?" Humphrey appeared to be amused by this request, obviously a mistake. He sheepishly reached into his pocket and produced a library card identifying him as Mason Landers.

Fred looked at it for several seconds. "Can I see your driver's license?"

Humphrey smiled again, a Reaganesque here-we-go-again smile. "Now I don't mean to be a pain, but I happen to know you can't ask to see a driver's license unless there's a matter concerning my driving or my vehicle."

Fred tilted his head sideways. "You drove here?" Humphrey nodded. "You plan on walking back?" Humphrey looked him in the eye while reaching his hand into his back pocket.

"Officer, maybe I could clear this up if you tell me what the problem is?" Fred continued to watch Humphrey's hand until he was sure it was a wallet that was removed.

"We have someone claiming that you aren't Mason Landers."

"I see." He nodded while turning the wallet over in his hands. "And is it a crime to not be Mason Landers?"

"That remains to be seen. But if you aren't Landers and you've been living in his house, driving his car, we'd be real interested in knowing that such use was authorized and that Mason Landers was safe and healthy." Humphrey looked around to Bryna and smiled. He hoped he projected the air of a man of patience being falsely accused, an incident they would all have a good laugh about later.

"I'm wondering who would make such a claim. There's no one in town who really knows me." On this cue Janice appeared from where she'd been listening in the next aisle. She smiled sweetly at Bryna.

"That would be me." By this time many of the staff and patrons noticed the confrontation and things quieted somewhat in that they stopped talking and started watching. "Last year, I happened to be getting gas and I knocked into this guy as I went to pay. He dropped his credit card and I had to flag him down to give it back to him. The name on the card was Mason Landers and he wasn't you." Humphrey grinned knowingly and sat on the table they'd been using. He hoped that it would convey that he was neither threatened by this inquiry nor threatening to make a run for it.

"So it didn't occur to any of you that he might be the impostor? That he might have stolen my stuff or even been someone that I let borrow my things?" He slipped his wallet back into his back pocket. Let's move along, nothing to see here.

Bryna nodded, pleased with the logic of that explanation. Janice looked momentarily horrified, the look followed quickly by determined, she would not let the matter rest on that note. Fred smiled and nodded in sympathy. "That can easily be resolved by showing me your driver's license."

Humphrey shook his head while reaching for his wallet again. He wasn't going to get out of this. As soon as he drove away he'd be stopped. He could refrain from driving, use the legality to make a point, and the weather was improving but he couldn't walk everywhere he needed to go even in this small town. He was sure this fashion plate librarian would press the issue and they would begin an investigation. There was just no way he was going to maintain his Mason cover and trying to do so only made him look more guilty of some imagined offense.

"This really isn't a police matter. I can assure you that there's nothing wrong with Mason Landers." Janice pumped her arm in triumph, Bryna merely tilted her head.

"I'm afraid we'll have to hear that from Mr. Landers."

"He isn't available."

"Uh huh. Isn't that convenient Mr...." he consulted the California driver's license that had been handed to him, "...Dixon? I'm afraid I'm going to have to ask you to come with me." Bryna stepped closer to Humphrey and grabbed hold of his upper arm. He bent that arm, flexing the bicep and placed his right hand atop hers. As he turned his head to look at her he lifted her hand off of his arm, holding it. He smiled at her with such a twinkle in his eye that he might have been Simon Templer the Saint, finally brought to ground. Suddenly Bryna turned to stare at Janice, her hair flying. Although she'd made no movement toward them Fred and Janice felt compelled to flinch away. With a huff she broke eye contact and turned back to Humphrey. He returned his wallet to his back pocket, Bryna still holding his other arm. He stepped away from her and followed Fred out of the library.

"So much for your good judgment of character, Bryna," Janice said as they watched the men leave. "I'll have to start watching who you favor and seek out the opposite."

"I've never made claims about my judgment, Janice, but I will stand by it. If this is still about Mark, I think it's time for you to get over it." Bryna looked around to see most of the staff and many patrons watching her. She walked away from Janice returning to her desk as casually as if another routine task had been completed. Only then did she look at the keys that he had slipped into her hand.

Janice, feeling like the center of attention after the others had walked away, decided her next move must be logical and benign. She headed into the stacks to replace the book she'd been using as cover and walked on further 'til she got to the gardening section. She could easily amuse herself for several minutes reading up on poisonous houseplants.

When she finally left she happened to meet Cicily at the door. Cicily was disoriented by meeting the librarian in the wrong place. "Oh, hi. Did you happen to see Mason Landers in there?"

"Why, no. No I didn't. I'm positive he isn't in there. He might not even be in town."

"Oh, do you think he went to Sioux Falls? He's done that before."

"There's no telling where he might have gone." Janice looked positively beatific.

"Well, I took your advice and confronted him this morning. He denied everything. He was quite forceful about it. I'm sure he's hiding something."

Janice really didn't want to become Cicily's confidant. "Well, you keep on it. I'm sure you'll get to the bottom of the story eventually."

Cicily was buoyed by this support, the first she'd received concerning the case since she'd gotten to town. Yes, she would persevere. "Thanks."

Chapter 32

After arranging coverage so she could take a longer lunch Bryna called the police station. "Mike, this is Bryna Halprin. Fred brought in a guy he picked up here at the library. What can you tell me?"

"He's here."

"Is he being charged?"

"Not yet."

"Has he been questioned? Does he need counsel?"

"He's refusing to answer any questions and says he doesn't want a lawyer until he's booked."

"I see. What are the chances that they'll let him go?"

"Don't know."

"But there's no indication of a crime."

"That's up to Steve."

"Will he be kept at the station?"

"He'll be kept here for questioning until some disposition is made. When he's charged he'll be taken to the county jail."

"Thanks, Mike."

Bryna was sure no one had seen the key exchange but what good did that do when she didn't know what he expected her to do with them? She assumed that there was something at the house that could help him or harm him. It couldn't be the car he wanted to keep them out of as it was already gone from the lot, probably hot-wired.

She drove to the house cognizant of the probability of either the police or Cicily Trimble watching. Thinking of what efforts she might take to keep from tipping them off, she parked her car in front of another house and looked carefully in the windows of all the houses she could see as she walked. Next door to the Landers house someone took that moment to leave. She kept walking as they drove away oblivious to her presence. A pickup whipped around the corner, radio blaring and zoomed down the street out of sight. By the time she stepped up to the front door, no one was around.

She feared that the cops would have been there and left someone behind still searching but there was no one inside. She nodded ferociously like the plastic dog in the back window of her late brother's Chevy. If she stayed away from windows she could look around without grossly announcing her presence.

What should she be looking for? What would she have in her own house that would be of help to anyone if she were unexpectedly locked away? An address book, possibly listing family or a lawyer? Maybe, but... She didn't list Mark under Husband or Ex-husband, didn't even put him under his last name. There he sat in the Ms, faceless, purposeless, rather fitting his new role. Even her dentist was just under Porter, not even a Dr. or DDS to distinguish him. If, however, this guy was more meticulous than she, an address book might be useful, but she hoped there would be something of quicker help.

She walked through the rooms to get oriented. The place was furnished as little more that a hotel suite with few personal touches, photos or papers; a bedroom, guestroom and bath, a kitchen, living room and dining area. There were notes on the refrigerator door, mostly unidentified phone numbers. In the basement, however, was an office with computer and a desk replete with papers; in files, in piles, in scattered disarray. And in all of this stuff how was she to know which things were Mason's and which were his stand-ins?

Bryna devised a systematic attack to eliminate as many useless papers as possible. As she got herself organized she was reminded that she'd assumed his place would smell of cinnamon. Whenever she'd been close to him he'd smelled of cinnamon and soap and a fragrance somewhat like gardenia, something familiar from her childhood.

There was a phone ringing faintly. The phone on the desk was not ringing but reflex led her to pick it up and hear the dial tone. The phone rang again. Bryna raced up the stairs listening for changes in the intensity. The phones she saw were not ringing. In the bedroom it was loudest. Nothing in sight. The bed itself was ringing. Bryna tossed the unmade bedding around until she caught sight of a cell phone. She tried a couple of buttons before finding the one that activated it. "Hello?"

"Oh. I'm sorry..." Bryna could sense a hang-up coming as if the embarrassment, regret and bewilderment were encapsulated in that hesitation after "Oh."

"No wait!! Are you calling for..." What was that name? "...Dixon? Mr. Dixon? A friend of Mason Landers?"

"Who is this?"

"So you do know him. Thank God. He needs help and I'm not sure who to contact."

"Who needs help?"

"Dixon. I'm sorry, I don't know his first name. He told us he was Mason Landers."

"And who are you?"

"Bryna Halprin. I'm a librarian."

"Ah. Yes. Where is he? Why are you answering his phone?"

"He's in jail..."

"What!!! Is he okay?"

"Yeah, sure. He'll be fine. See, apparently Janice, uh this other librarian, figured out that he wasn't who he said he was and told the cops that they should make sure he hadn't killed Mason and taken over his identity. He, Dixon, said he couldn't verify that Mason is unharmed so they took him in."

This one knew a lot, but was it enough? Jodie realized that there was no way she could be sure that this was the woman he had trusted, nor that, if she was, she could still be trusted. Oh well. "His name is Humphrey. He and Mason went to college together. Mason apparently works overseas a lot and is often unavailable, so he let Hum stay there for a while. It was all arranged by phone. If any harm has come to Mason, Hum had nothing to do with it. What about Cicily Trimble?"

"You know about her, too? Hmm. Who are you, by the way?"

The caller considered for several moments, obviously conflicted. "I'm his agent."

"I'm sorry, it seems I know nothing at all about him. What does he do? Why does he need an agent?"

Ooo, Jodie's apprehensions were churning. "He's a screenwriter."

"Ah, so he must have been doing research for a story."

"Yes."

"Why here?"

Jodie hesitated. How rude should she be to this person? How forthcoming? "He just needed to get away from distractions to do some work and Mason offered him the use of his house."

"So why was he passing himself off as Mason?"

Because he's an idiot, she thought. "He didn't want to be recognized. That's immaterial. How can we get him out of jail?"

"They want proof that Mason is okay. We need to get in touch with him."

"I don't know anything about that. There's a number that Hum called and left a message at. After awhile Mason would call him back."

"And you don't know what it is? He didn't give you any emergency numbers?"

"No. He had it memorized. He didn't foresee any reason why I would have to contact Mason."

"What about where Mason works, his family, other friends?"

"No one knows who he works for and I don't know anyone else who knew him. Hum said that none of his friends have any better contact with him. It was the number or nothing. Anyway, Mason told him recently that he would be out of contact for months."

"Good gravy, what does Mason do, anyway?"

"They don't know."

"Great. Just great. As far as the cops are concerned a question has been raised. Even if there is no other evidence against Ma... Humphrey, the cops aren't going to be able to just forget it without some confirmation that no crime was committed. They're very picky about this kind of thing. A number of women have gone missing lately so they're especially wary."

"Perhaps if I talk to them, verify his story."

"He hasn't given them a story. He gave them his ID and hasn't said another word."

"Are you sure?"

"I talked to the cops."

"Listen, you know that town, what's likely to happen?"

"He's safe, if that's what you mean. They're holding him at the police station not at the county jail. Either way he'll be treated well. But even if we're able to get him released, they'll be watching him."

"Okay. I'll see what I can do." Jodie hung up. Bryna didn't think the conversation was over. She wandered back downstairs to the office. Sooner or later the cops would come to look over these same things. If there was a clue, she should probably find it first. Most of the stuff was financially oriented. She started sorting through the papers making piles of receipts, statements. There were things that were in Humphrey's name but they had been sent to a PO Box in Sioux Falls.

She started studying the Mason papers first, he was the one she was looking for after all. But there was nothing of substance that wasn't based in Brookings. Then again, why would there be? He didn't need to contact himself. So, with little further ado she found some scratch paper and noted down the numbers on Humphrey's cell phone bill. Then she proceeded to hide these papers where someone might if they felt they were being followed by a strange woman.

Then there was the computer. She was familiar with computers but had never had to look for something on someone else's PC. If Humphrey were really in trouble the police would surely look there for evidence. She considered for a few seconds before turning it on. Starting at the top of the directory she began looking at files. Most of them turned out to be password controlled. Most that weren't were innocuous and dated prior to Humphrey's arrival. She decided to not take the time to read the files to see if there was anything incriminating. For one thing she didn't have the time, for another she wasn't sure what would be considered incriminating.

When she found a file that Humphrey had saved she saved a copy to two blank floppy discs, checked that the save was clean then deleted it from the hard drive. When she'd deleted all of his files she changed the computer date, went back to one of Mason's open files and judging by the file size saved it under different names dozens of times, theorizing that this data would overlay the data she'd deleted and prevent an expert from undeleting it. Just before turning it off she remembered to change the date back.

One disc she hid along with the phone bills. The other she took with her.

Before she left she went back to the bedroom and opened the closet. Nope. No cinnamon. It must be him.

Chapter 33

After work Bryna parked in one of the quick spots in front of the police station. "Excuse me," she said to the dispatcher who was obviously sorting some papers for filing, "I found these keys at the library. I believe they might belong to a man that the police brought in earlier today."

"His name?"

"Uh, I think the officer called him Dixon. He was using the facilities of Mason Landers so the case might be under his name." She waited as the woman checked a list, flicked the mike on the intercom, summoned Fred and returned to her task.

Bryna looked benignly out the window of the door while Fred talked to the dispatcher and got the story about the keys. "Why did it take you so long to bring in the keys?"

She gave him a 'well, duh' look and replied, "I had to finish my shift."

"You could have called and had us pick up the keys."

"I would have thought you would consider that a frivolous use of your limited police power." He looked at her a few seconds to evaluate her sincerity, not noticing the double meaning.

"Well, thanks. I'll see that the investigators get them."

He had turned to go when Bryna called him back. "I was wondering if I could talk to Mr. Dixon. I talked to Mike who said he wasn't making any statements." Fred was extremely suspicious about this development. "So I thought maybe I could talk to him, since he's just sitting there." Fred thought about it for several seconds before leading her into the back part of the station. He left her outside of an office while he whispered with someone inside then led her further along and into a room where Humphrey sat alone at a table. The door was closed behind her. There was no mirror, but they both suspected some kind of monitoring device.

"Your agent called."

"Jodie? Called who?"

She mouthed the words slowly, hoping he could read lips. 'She called on your cell phone. I would have brought it but...' He nodded grudgingly. Aloud she finally said, "You."

"What did she say?"

"Not much. Mainly that she didn't know how to get ahold of Mason."

"Good. I don't want Mason brought into this."

"But they won't let it go until they know he's all right." Her eyes pleaded with him to relent.

"Maybe, but it's important that he not be exposed." He winced at his choice of words, a regrettable implication.

"What is he hiding?"

"I don't know, but I intend to protect his privacy. What was it with that other librarian anyway?"

"Janice? You probably met her at the university library."

"Yeah, I remember her. I've seen her around. She'd been very helpful, seemed so nice. But today...she was so ruthless. She was really getting a charge out of turning me in."

"She'll tell herself (and everyone else) that it was her civic duty to expose whatever nefarious motives you had for impersonating Mason Landers. But I suspect it had little to do with you."

"I'm in custody, it feels like it had to do with me." He sat back in the chair, arms folded across his chest, the dejected prisoner.

"I know and I'm sorry about that. I think mainly she was attacking me."

"Why?"

"Some time ago she started living with my ex-husband. Mark's a very dashing and clever fellow. He turns a lot of heads. She thought I'd been an idiot to let him go. For some time she quietly lorded it over me that she'd claimed what I had not been able to keep. It took her awhile to discover what a jerk he was, is, and at that point she blamed me for not having warned her. Janice doesn't deal well with things getting out of her control."

"Great. So now I'm in her control, that should make her real happy."

She laughed and shook her head. "No, I doubt that Janice will ever be happy. In any case, Humphrey, I really think you should tell them the whole story."

"What whole story?"

"What you're doing here, why you were passing yourself off as Mason Landers."

"I can't."

"Listen, your agent said you don't even know what Mason does so you can't give anything away about him, you won't be disclosing any confidences because you don't have any."

He lowered his voice, exaggerating the mouthing of the words. "What about Cicily Trimble?"

Bryna replied in equally low tones, "She's looking for Mason."

"Exactly."

She resumed normal volume, "Humphrey, the longer you evade them the more they'll suspect you're up to no good. They'll imagine worse things about you than whatever it is you're hiding from them. And, they might go public with your case hoping to get information from someone else.

"Isn't there someone else I can call to help you? Friends, family?"

"Not really."

"No friends?"

His defenses turned him into a little boy falsely accused. "I have friends. Just no one who could help in this situation."

"No girlfriend for moral support?"

"No. And I'm not on such good terms with my old girlfriends."

"Ah," she whispered, "you beat them."

"Of course not!" He looked up to see that she was smiling, he smiled too, realizing she was just joking with him. "No. Jodie says they all leave me because I tend to incorporate them into characters I'm writing. I don't see it. I mean, if I'm going out with a model and I write a model into a script, it doesn't mean that... Okay, I may start with the basics of someone I know but then I change them, I make them look different, I make them smarter or dumber or nastier. The point is that I make the character fit the role she needs to play in the plot. It's nothing personal."

"Apparently it's personal to the people you use." He watched her.

"You think Jodie's right, don't you? Well, if I do, I don't mean to."

"And you don't mean not to. The point is that the people probably feel that you haven't considered them at all, their sensibilities, their reactions to being recognizable. You don't see them for what they really are. The result is that you don't have close friends."

He didn't know how to reply and she knew it. She leaned in closer. "Listen," she whispered, "was there something particular you wanted me to do," then she mouthed 'at your house?'

"Oh, I don't know. I guess I just didn't want them to have an easy time of it." He used sign language to indicate his phone. 'Where?'

She mouthed 'My car'.

"So I guess there's nothing I can do for you?"

He lowered his head to hide the silly grin. "No. But thanks."

Having listened in on the conversation between Bryna and Humphrey as passively as if it were a chat by the coffeepot, Ace Bennett gleaned little of use and proceeded with his normal investigative procedures.

Chapter 34

Humphrey was dozing off when the opening of the door stirred him. As he looked up he saw the officer, who was reaching out to wake him, stop and step back.

Ace Bennett followed Mike into the room and sat across from Humphrey spreading papers from a file folder before him. "Okay, here's what we know, even without your help. You got here in January and started passing yourself off as Mason Landers. You haven't caused any trouble, minded your own business, paid your bills. You are indeed Humphrey Dixon. You're a screenwriter of some apparent repute living in Santa Monica. Seems you've had a little trouble back there so you came here to" he consulted the papers pointedly, making it clear that he doubted the official explanation, "get some work done.

"Now, usually when there's a murder involving a stalking situation it's a stalkee that's killed or the stalkee ends up killing the stalker, in self defense of course. There you were out in LA being stalked. Let's just suppose it was Landers who was stalking you and you knew it."

"What?" That brought Humphrey out of his slump.

"I doubt that you would have reported it unless you were thereby establishing an alibi." Ace maintained an air of bored indifference. It all seemed to be perfectly logical to him whatever scenario he happened to be spinning. He would never admit to anyone that it was a frame of mind he'd developed after seeing it used effectively on a number of difference police dramas. It had been a whim to begin with, to prove his assumption that such a technique would not really work. In fact it didn't work in all cases, but he'd been ashamedly surprised at how many it did work on.

"P-lease."

"Yeah," Mike was getting excited about the possibilities of this line of thinking. "report that you don't know who it is, kill him, claim you're still being stalked and come here claiming he let you. I like that, it fits."

"He did let me."

Ace resumed his speculation. "But let's suppose you didn't know it was him until you killed him. I believe I know a psychiatrist who would argue that you were in denial from the shock of having killed your friend and you came here to assume his identity and atone for his loss."

"There is no loss. Call the LA police. Did you call them? They know who it was that was stalking me. His name is Horace Ellers."

"Evans." Hum pointed at Ace acknowledging the correct name as well as his having done the obvious. "But there's no real reason to dismiss the possibility that Evans and Landers were working together." Humphrey shook his head and rubbed his forehead. He was inclined to laugh at the absurdity of it. A mock 'You got me' was tempting but the pictures in his head told him sarcasm and confessions don't mix well. "There's something strange about this Evans case isn't there? They wouldn't go into too many details."

"Evans is supposed to have been killed."

"Ah yes, they did mention that. And you wrote the movie. You know Mike, I wouldn't be surprised if this Evans and Landers are one and the same, an alias for the other. Or maybe Evans really was killed and Landers took over his identity. Has anyone ever seen them together?"

Humphrey yawned. He was truly tired but as a display of boredom it was enough to put Bennett off his speculation game. "We'd like to know what you're hiding, why you refuse to talk. But I don't think you're going to tell me, are you? Well, I suppose it's better than making up some lies that you have to keep straight." With that he gathered the papers he'd not bothered to consult and left the room.

For fifteen minutes Humphrey sat and yawned trying to remember all the suppositions and how he could counter them if it came to that.

"We're releasing you," announced the district attorney as he stepped into the doorway without looking up from the papers in his hands. "At this point we feel we don't need to be paying for your keep. That doesn't mean we're through with you. You are not to leave town." He continued to read the papers as he turned and led Humphrey down the hall, all the way explaining the terms of release like a litany.

"You are being released into the nominal custody of Orinda Waters." Humphrey's brow went wrinkled but he kept walking. "...This is your notification..." without turning he held out behind him a paper which Humphrey reached for mechanically. "...that a search warrant was issued and..." he checked his watch, "...is about to be implemented. You will not be allowed to stay in the house alone until they are done and they won't be done tonight. It was fortunate for you that Ms Halprin 'found' your keys. Since you are unemployed we'll expect to find you at home, so to speak. Should you choose to spend any large blocks of time elsewhere we would..." The rest of the spiel droned off into background percussion as they reached the front office and he saw Orinda and Bryna rise from where they'd been waiting. They were both dressed in jeans, sweaters and sports jackets under down coats, Orinda in shades of blue, Bryna in browns and greens.

Bryna was several inches taller, hair and glasses were completely different but the eyes, the deep blue, the crinkles at the corners, he'd been an idiot not to see it before. "This is your mother who loves symbols?"

The women took a quick look at each other, Orinda raising her eyebrows at having been described so. "Yeah." They said nothing more as Humphrey was supplied with his coat and other items that had been taken from him. Orinda was given instructions and papers to sign while Bryna helped Humphrey with his coat. This simple task was complicated by his unwillingness to take his eyes off of her. It was nearly midnight when they left. There was no one about and it had begun to snow.

Chapter 35

They piled into the front seat of Orinda's pickup. "Why are they releasing me to you?"

Orinda let the wipers clear the windshield, having wiped the side window and mirror before she'd gotten in with the swipe of her padded mitten. "Because I asked them to."

"Just like that?"

"They trust my instincts."

"Okay. Whatever. There's obviously stuff I've missed here." He turned to Bryna who'd pushed him into the middle. "Why didn't you tell me Orinda was you mother?"

"It never occurred to me. Would it have made any difference?"

"Well, no, of course not. It's just that I've tried hard to limit my personal contacts here only to find that... they've been conspiring behind..."

Bryna was busy watching the side streets for traffic problems. "I'd hardly call it conspiring."

"No, we were just comparing notes. No conspiracy here." Orinda smiled broadly at the prospect of being part of a conspiracy.

"Okay. I give. Now what? There is no evidence for them to find, yet they won't let me off the hook until they find something."

"They've been searching your house, uh, Mason's house. They're still there. You'll have to stay with me tonight. They won't let you back in until they've found everything useful."

"Orinda, there is nothing useful. I didn't do anything. All I want to keep from them is how to get ahold of Mason."

"I wouldn't worry about that if I were you." At that he turned and looked at Bryna for clues to her suspicious statement. She smiled. "I looked through the papers in the basement. I found your phone bills. I hid them. I also found some files on the computer and got rid of them."

"What!!!!" He might have hit the ceiling if he hadn't been strapped in.

"I saved them on floppy first. Geez, Humphrey, chill! Do you think I'd be stupid enough to just destroy information? Credit!" If she could have reached inside her coat, a Picard-like tug of her shirtfront would have been appropriate.

"Sorry. Sorry. It's just that I had two months of my work on there. What did you do with them?"

"I made two copies. One of them I hid with the papers and the other I took home."

"Why hide it, why not just take it with you?"

"Because it's a crime to remove evidence from a crime scene."

Humphrey's level of exasperation had risen since leaving the station, since he'd placed himself among people who he thought he could trust. Why did they not just accept his word? "It isn't a crime scene."

"Granted, but I'd rather not be booked in the first place." She squirmed to reach her pocket and pulled from it a small spiral notebook and pen. Handing it to him she said, "I thought you'd probably be going nuts if they didn't let you write." He took it, appraising it gratefully and slipped it into his jacket.

They'd reached Orinda's house in an older section of town where the houses were grander and mostly owned by university people. Hum was shown directly to a guest room upstairs and asked not to leave, a technicality of Orinda's custody agreement. It was well after midnight and they were all tired. They'd gotten him a burger at the station and he was still hungry but he didn't press it, he had some notes to get down while they were fresh.

They awoke to four inches on top of the four that had accumulated during the day. Since it was Sunday the plows would have started a little later than usual. Orinda was up and cooking breakfast when Humphrey wandered down. He'd taken a little time first to look around for details he could use in his writing.

"We won't be getting out for a while and neither will the cops. You might be here 'til tomorrow."

"I'm grateful for what you and Bryna have done for me. You don't really know me, have no reason to assume that I'm innocent..."

"Sure there is."

"Really?"

"Humphrey, isn't it? I bet someone calls you Free. Am I right?"

Hesitantly... "Yeah. A few."

She nodded as she flipped her pancakes. "That picture is of Bryna when she was in high school. She was very good with horses, but her heart wasn't in it, she did it for her father." Hum was confused. He was looking past Orinda to the far wall. She could not have known what he was looking at.

But she did. What was it with these two?

"You have a lovely home. Mason's place is very sparsely furnished because he doesn't stay there often. I'd forgotten how comforting things could be."

"It isn't the things that are comforting, it's the spirit that lingers from the placing." She didn't ask him what he wanted, she just made breakfast. "In the fall here we have a home tour. People with exceptional homes open them up to the public who pay for tickets. Beforehand someone comes around and helps the owners make strategic changes. Ostensibly it's for the protection of objects that could be damaged or filched, but sometimes people turn over the whole thing to them to redecorate, temporarily. And only when there's a serious need. They come out looking like show pieces. They're lovely, picture perfect. But in every one of those major redecorations I've seen, the owners decide not to incorporate the changes. They don't feel right, they weren't placed there with the genuine spirit of caring that their own things were. Everything looked perfect, but in real life it's the imperfect things that distinguish."

He should have offered to help with breakfast but he was engrossed in digesting the things Orinda had placed around her. Helping only occurred to him when she told him to sit and he saw that everything was ready.

"Free, where does your friend Mason usually live, if he doesn't have his personal things here?"

"I'm not sure. He has a place in LA, but I've never been there. I don't hear from him often, I suspect he doesn't spend any more time there than here."

"Bryna said you were actually a screenwriter?"

How did she know that? Oh, yeah, Jodie. "Yes."

"Hard business to break into." Hum was surprised that she would be aware of the subtleties of his industry. "She tells me you've had some success." Now how the hell did Bryna know that?

"I've been lucky. And I have a good agent." Hum was still undecided about how much it was safe to tell anyone. "However, I've never had the power to get someone out of jail. What's up with that?"

Orinda looked up at him, fork poised for insertion. What up? LA gutter slang? Who knew? "I talked to the police chief. I explained that I felt certain that you were harmless. He accepted my judgment." There was a noise at the door. It was Bryna. She came in stomping and sat to take off her ski boots.

"They've got the primary streets cleared. You're going to have to go to the shop."

"You're open on Sunday? I never noticed."

"People like to visit the hospital after church so they often stop by the flower shop before church. One of the assistants usually has to come in at 9:30 just so there's someone there." Bryna had cleaned the snowdrops off of her glasses and sat down like a coveting cat to watch them eat.

"Damned efficiency. Beginning of winter they wouldn't have gotten to the streets by Tuesday. Why don't you finish my breakfast while I get ready?" Orinda left the room quickly.

"I'll come with you," Hum offered as she left and turned back to find Bryna digging into the last pancake.

"Fine. You can help us push the truck out if we get stuck." She looked up from where she leaned over the plate, syrup dripping from her lip, and gave him an exaggerated grin. A tongue slipped out on retrieval duty. "Know anything about flowers?"

"Not from personal experience, but I've been learning a lot lately. Right now I think you'd be better off using me for my brute strength." He flexed his biceps with obvious ineffectuality.

Bryna smiled. "Hm. So much to learn about Humphrey."

"Do you always spend your weekends helping your mother?"

"Nope," she said around a full mouth. Swallow. "I need to keep an eye on you."

He looked around to where Orinda had gone upstairs. "But, they released me in her..."

"I'm the one who told her you needed to be sprung. You're as much my responsibility as hers."

He put his napkin down and leaned back. "I appreciate being out but I would have been all right. It's not like they were going to beat me or anything." His brow suddenly wrinkled. "Unless..." He inexplicable imagined being staked down to the desert floor next to an anthill

"No! No. They're good people. However, I suspect they contract with the dorm for food. You're better off with us. Besides, she's upstairs calling her staff telling them not to go to any trouble to get to work."

"How do you know that? She didn't say anything. Do you two have some secret signals?"

"Foreign concept called logic. You'll get used to it." Why, he wondered, did she find it so easy to tease him? Had she been talking more to Jodie?

Orinda swept in dressed in a huge Aran sweater that spilled out the sides of her overalls. Humphrey jumped up and hurried upstairs to get his coat, then down to pull on his boots while they stood waiting for him in silence.

"Free?" asked Orinda tolerantly, "don't you think your boots will get uncomfortable if you wear them indoors all day? Why don't you check in the closet and see if anything fits?"

Puzzled, he returned to the guestroom. The closet was full of clothes; men's, women's, large, small, pants, shirts, skirts, coats, boots, sneakers, assorted packages of socks, panties and shorts. He sat at the foot of the bed in awe. Quickly he looked through the running shoes found a size a little bigger than his own and took a little extra time to change his underwear. They were still waiting when he returned, shoes in hand.

The truck had no trouble getting to the store. Bryna insisted on handling the snow blower herself. Hum watched her admiringly and was stunned when a customer drove in not two minutes after she'd finished. They didn't let him do anything requiring skill but they kept him busy nonetheless.

Close to noon Cicily Trimble showed up. She didn't ask for anything but they knew she was looking for Mason. Fortunately he'd noticed her car and had time to hide in the back. After that he was leery of coming out of the back room. He decided to confide in them what Jodie had found out about the weather girl. "Ahhh," they both said and nodded knowingly. This made him laugh to a point he found hard to stop. He wasn't sure himself whether it was out of delight at having found these unusual women or frustration at being trapped with them.

After the post-church rush of seven people things slowed down considerably. They talked about places he should see in South Dakota: the Black Hills, of course, the Badlands, the Mammoth site, their own McCrory Gardens. They all sounded interesting but he chose not to mention that if things worked out he wouldn't be around much longer.

He noticed halfway into the afternoon that they hadn't asked him about himself, while he had asked them for many personal details none of which they had refused to answer. He knew them both to be curious people. And Bryna, he felt sure, would not hesitate to ask. Either she didn't trust him to tell her the truth about himself or she was respecting his privacy. He wasn't used to that sentiment. They came upon him at that point in his musing and found him grinning. He couldn't explain and they didn't ask him. Instead he asked about Janice.

"It doesn't feel right that she should be able to have me locked up for no good reason."

"You'd like to get back at her, teach her a lesson." Orinda was taking spent roses out of arrangements. With the snow they wouldn't be getting in a new shipment for a while.

"Yeah."

"The thing with Janice is that she may learn from something but it's never the lesson you expect her to learn. For instance, there's a workshop that we have here now and then. She usually manages it. One year she assigned a large part to a guy who proved to be completely incompetent at that task. She said she thought it would be a growth opportunity for him, oblivious to the distress it caused.

Next time, instead of trying to match up the talents of the people available with the tasks to be done, she again assigned people to unsuitable tasks and just made the tasks smaller so that the problems were spread out over more people."

"So you're saying there's no way of getting back at her."

Bryna stepped closer to him with obvious glee and asked with hopes of collusion, "What would you suggest?"

Humphrey stopped to think. "Oh, public humiliation is always fun." The look on his face reflected the various pictures that ran through his head. Janice pilloried in the Burger King parking lot. Janice demoted to stall maintenance at the campus cow barn. Janice in basic training, a raw recruit forever. "How about a billboard? Janice's face and a veiled reference to false accusations. Something that would cut her down to size."

"She'd turn martyr on you. She's quite good at that." Orinda nodded in agreement with Bryna.

"Something to strip her of control, memo to her boss…"

Bryna could see from his eyes that he was warming up to that topic, but shook her head emphatically. "Now that might be dangerous. Remember she's very big on revenge."

"Ah, yes."

Orinda, being no saint, had been enjoying the mind game as well, but felt compelled, as a mother, to point out, "There's the rub, you see. As satisfying as retaliation might seem, there's always a price. It's always the best course not to stoop to someone else's level. Justice is one thing, but getting back is best left to the fates."

Bryna rolled her eyes skyward.

"The plan can be hatched," Orinda went on to explain, "as long as it isn't carried out. That can be quite cathartic actually." Hum looked at Bryna for some reading on her mother's sincerity.

"Psych major," was all she said on that. On the other matter she let her imagination fly. "What about if we hire someone to come in and say he's Mason and get on her case about blowing his cover?"

"She says she saw Mason."

"Oh yeah. We could get some people to pose as a TV news crew and storm into the library demanding answers."

"I like that."

"We could get someone to follow her, someone cute so she won't be sure if he's interested in her or out to get her." Humphrey stared at her until she realized that was too close to reality. "Okay, what about telling her she's to appear on one of the local news talk shows. Arrange when she should show up, what she should wear, send a confirmation letter. Then she shows up and they don't have a clue."

"Humiliating, yes, but no one but the station people would see it."

"True, but we could make sure her staff knew she was going." Orinda looked askance at her daughter. Although she, too, was having fun at this speculation, it seemed that Bryna was way too good at this and getting too much vicarious thrill from the exercise.

He thought of people he knew at the national talk shows. "Hey, if you want to go that way, I could probably get some letterhead from Jesse or Jenny. I do have connections."

"Ha! Wouldn't that be great?! I can just see her eating it up. Ah. Too bad we can't go through with it." She took a few deep breaths then went over to kiss Orinda. "You're right, Mother, that was very cathartic." She returned to where she was winding ribbon, stopping as she passed Humphrey to ask close to his ear, "And how was it for you?"

He laughed. "I guess I really needed that."

During another lull one of Bryna's favorite songs came on the radio that played in the background and she began moving to it. Hum stepped up and took her hand leading her into an unstructured two-step that had them all laughing well into the next song.

Not long before time to close, no one had been in for an hour, they'd each been busy with their tasks, Humphrey voiced his musings. "I don't suppose you have any dirt on her."

"On Janice?"

"Yeah. Something from those bridge parties of yours." Bryna looked up at Orinda. "Something that would sink her reputation."

Orinda answered from across the room where she gazed out the small window at the snow on the roof next door. "I don't know, Free, it's hard to sink anything around here. Especially a reputation. People are pretty forgiving."

"I'd say it's harder in LA. People with money and power get away with all manner of evil out there. I'm not saying we actually leak anything, I'm just wondering if there's anything to leak. Like, I don't know, maybe a gambling habit, maybe she likes little boys, maybe she's a closet dominatrix."

He saw Orinda whip her head around to glare at Bryna, to warn her not to speak. "Omygod! That's it, isn't it? Omygod. I was just joking, grabbing at..." better not let on why he'd thought of that particular predilection, "but that's it. It fits. The prim flip side, the need for control." He was pacing, overwhelmed by the rush. Bryna put down her work and calmly wiped the dirt off her hands. She walked to him and grabbed him by the shoulders. Strong, firm shoulders, she noticed subliminally.

"Humphrey, you will not ever speak of this."

With her arms already nearly around him he wrapped her in a hug and, laughing, picked her up off the floor which she tried hard to find annoying. "How do you know about a thing like that? Does everybody know? Is this what really comes out at bridge?" He would have to revise his image of a commando bridge club, it was clearly too tame. There was some serious information gathering here.

Bryna shook her head and ambled back to her work. "Why do you think she left Mark? What kind of partner is a disappointment to someone like that?"

"I don't know, I didn't do the research. A wimp? You didn't say why you left him. You said he was a jerk but that doesn't seem like grounds. I thought maybe he was abusive or a drunk."

She shook her head. "What they don't want is a rival." She watched the thoughts run across his face ending in distasteful puzzlement. He saw a leather-clad, whip-wielding, Amazon in four inch spike heels poised to fight. Panning around to see the opponent, a similarly clad man in a blonde wig and pink boa looked disdainfully at the prospects. He shook his head to clear the image. Bryna, sure that he'd gone off-track, relented to explain. "Mark was just as domineering. Not at first. It was something that came out as the relationship lost its initial glow. When they found that neither would submit they were both angry to have been fooled by the image."

This made sense to Humphrey until he remembered that Bryna had also left Mark. He backed off, mentally and physically.

She saw the look in his eyes and gave him a light whack on the arm. "Noo. Not me. I left him because he thought so little of me. He really thought I would submit. There was no love in him for me."

Humphrey absently rubbed his arm as he turned to walk back to where he'd been sitting. He looked over and saw Orinda working as though nothing special had happened. "Well, I'm glad to hear that. I mean I'm not glad you had to go through that. I'm sure it was very unpleasant. I'm just glad, you know, that you aren't...that way.

"And as for Janice," he started grinning again, "it's too bad we can't use something like that. But you're right, we can't. And I won't speak of it. I promise." But the grin remained firm.

Back at Orinda's while he waited for her to make dinner, despite his offer to help, he remembered that his cell phone had been turned off. He found it and immediately called Jodie.

"Are you okay?"

"Yes. Yes, I'm fine. I'm not in jail."

"You jerk! I was worried about you! I would have called the cops there but I didn't know if they knew about me."

"I'm sorry Jodes, I've been so busy I just didn't think." He sat on the side of the bed and looked out the window at the snow, the patterns cast by the streetlights, the different colors made by light from the window downstairs.

"Yeah, I should be used to being ignored until you need me."

"Jodie, I'm really sorry. Really. They released me last night into the custody of the florist. It was late and they wouldn't let me go back to Mase's so I'm staying in her guest room. Jodie, it turns out that the florist is the librarian's mother. We spent the day at her shop and we just got back. I haven't really had a chance to be alone."

"Don't try to snow me Humphrey, I know you just forgot."

When would he ever learn? "Yeah, I did."

"Gee, honesty. I guess your incarceration hasn't been a total loss. Are you coming back now?"

"No. I haven't been cleared. They still want proof that Mason is alive. And Cicily is still around and looking for me."

"Well, they've set the sting for Tuesday." Gosh, too bad she forgot to tell him that she'd called off the substitute part of the plan.

Hum heard someone coming up the stairs. "Good. Jodie, I have to go now. I promise I'll call you back."

The dinner of quiche and a savory potato soup was interrupted by a call from the cops. They wanted to confirm that Humphrey was still around and to inform him that they had confiscated his computer. They were still looking at his car and someone would drop it by at Orinda's the next day. That reminded Humphrey of the files Bryna said she'd saved on a disk for him. She promised to bring the disk the next day so that he could be sure they were all there.

Mondays Orinda took time off. She had Humphrey help her move some things around the house. Mid-morning Bryna showed up with the disk. She'd called earlier to ask what program he'd been using. It turned out to be something Orinda didn't have on her PC. Bryna offered to temporarily load a copy from the library so that he could ease his mind. She proceeded to access the files to make sure that they converted cleanly and in glancing at them casually she discovered that there was familiar information in several of the files. Too late Humphrey focused on what she was doing, saw the mistake, claimed it wasn't all that important and told her to close them down.

"No. I'd like to hear your explanation of this. Mother!"

His face turned red, his heart was racing. "Bryna, now don't get carried away. This isn't what you think."

Orinda strolled into the office wiping her hands on a towel.

"These files of Humphrey's are all about a florist."

"Really?" She stepped forward to get a better look. Hum tried to edge Bryna out of the way so that he could keep the two of them from reading any details.

He miscalculated Bryna's self-defense instincts and training. After feeling a hand on his shoulder and a foot behind his knee he found himself flat on his back staring up at an amused and triumphant victor. This time when the eyes opened wide he saw the look; predator, but he didn't have the presence of mind to recognize it.

"Geez, Bryna." Hum sounded ego-wounded, like a brother betrayed. "It's no big deal." His mind conjured up Robin of Locksley, doubled over after being whacked in the crotch, saying 'Hello Marion'. Humphrey the conjurer screamed 'Noooo! That's the wrong symbolism for this relationship.'

Orinda sat at the computer. "Free, this is information about running a flower shop, and about the old lady who runs it, and about the town. This is my life. Humphrey, you're turning me into a movie?"

"No." Humphrey stared up at Bryna, poised to disable him should he try to intercept her mother. He laid back flat on the rug, a beautiful old Persian in rose with tiny flowers. The ceiling, he now saw, was a pale blue. "Look, I came here to work, to come up with an idea for a new script and do enough research to make it believable. The best idea I came up with was about someone who wins a lot of money and decides to give it away anonymously only to have some con man come in and try to swindle her out of it. I thought of all that before I went looking for suitable atmosphere. The character is not going to be like you. I swear."

"Like your last dozen girlfriends?" Bryna spoke with unusual quiet.

"Jodie doesn't know what she's talking about." Bryna looked at Orinda. From where he lay it seemed that some kind of confirmation had been rendered. Bryna stepped back, accepting his prostrate passivity. He took this as a clue that he could get up.

"Look, I can show how there will be changes."

"That won't be necessary, Free. I think you better go now." Orinda sounded drained. She rose and returned to the kitchen. Bryna raised her eyebrows at him.

He reached over to retrieve the disk and headed for the stairs. "Where did you hide the other stuff?"

"In your utility room there's a section of exposed insulation. Check behind there." Slowly he mounted the stairs. Bryna went to commiserate with her mother. In about 5 minutes Hum returned all bundled up.

"I'll return the underwear I borrowed once I've washed it." Bryna got a grocery bag for him to carry things in.

"Your car hasn't come yet. I'll drive you."

"No. I'll walk. I need the exercise. I'm sorry Orinda, it really isn't what you think."

Chapter 36

It had taken Humphrey almost an hour to get back to Mason's. It was probably less than a couple miles but there were sections of his route that hadn't been plowed yet and many places where the plowed ridges blocked the sidewalk. He'd hoped he could have come up with a plan along the way but his mind had gone numb. He sat in the recliner and stared not even bothering with the TV. The computer was gone. He really didn't feel like working on the story anyway. He sat there for hours running it all through his head again trying to find where he'd gone wrong, what he could do to get out of this mess.

Chapter 37

Janice thought about it all weekend and decided not to mention her part in the Saturday ambush until confronted. She was going for the modesty angle, knowing full well that the word would have gotten around at church gatherings, grocery lines and mall encounters by the time she got to work. Various people did mention it in passing and she was required to give a full account at a busier than normal break.

"So once you realized that it was an impersonator why did you think to call the police?" It didn't seem to Clarie like the most logical step.

"Well, just look at the way he was acting. Completely confident that his cover was secure, no means of support, not concerned that he wasn't acting at all like the real guy, and then this woman shows up looking for the real Mason. She expected him to be here and he wasn't. So where was he? And if he was supposed to be here, why was this Dixon person so confident? There was too much that didn't fit, too much of a chance for foul play."

"I couldn't just ignore it. And it was obvious that Bryna Halprin had been taken in by him. Why I'd never forgive myself if anything happened to Bryna."

Kate was truly disappointed. "Gee, now what is that woman going to do? It won't be nearly as much fun around here."

Cicily had not found Mason anywhere for the rest of the weekend. She had assumed he'd gone to see a girlfriend or someone. When he wasn't back Monday morning she decided to ask about him at his regular haunts. When she stopped at the library and didn't find him she asked the girl at the desk if Mason Landers had been in yet, she told her he hadn't.

She hesitated to do so but eventually decided to return to the drug store. Boldly she admitted to the clerk, "I was here on Saturday and confronted a man, tall, blond, glasses?"

"Yes, I remember him."

"Has he been in since? Like today?"

"No, he hasn't. And it looked to me like he didn't want to talk to you. Perhaps you ought to leave him be."

"I'm afraid I can't. He's an integral part of a case I'm working on. His name is Mason Landers and I must speak with him." Cicily waited for her plea to sway the clerk and convince her to give him up.

"Excuse me, I couldn't help hearing." Cicily turned to see a plain looking, dark-haired woman who'd been reading the labels of some products nearby. Cicily was annoyed by the interruption, but given the site, she felt it prudent to deign to listen to her. "Why are you looking for Mason Landers?"

"Do you know where he is?"

"No. Why is it so important to you?"

"If you must know I have reason to believe he is involved in a number of cases of industrial cover-up. I've been watching him for some time. I chose what turned out to be an unfavorable time to confront him and now he seems to have run."

"You've been following him? What does he look like, maybe I've seen him?"

"Oh I'm sure you have. He gets around a lot. He wears a green parka and a Dodgers' cap."

"Yes. I remember him. Who did you say you were working for?"

"I didn't say. I'm a reporter from California."

"A reporter, how exciting! And you came all the way here to check out this story?"

Cicily had been pushed to her civil limit. "Yes, it's been a real treat. Do you know where he is?"

"No, I haven't seen him today. Sorry." Cicily was not surprised. The first person to show interest in her quest and she didn't know anything.

Chapter 38

"Ms White, there's a man here with a spec script. I explained to him our policy but he insists on speaking with you. He says it will only take a few moments of your time. Is there any chance you can squeeze him in?" Jodie had been flipping through some papers while listening to Dolly. One hand had forcefully wadded a page into a tight ball and was poised at just the angle, discerned from thousands of practice shots, to make a basket in the bin beside the door. It hung there motionless. Squeeze him in? The boss hated the picture invoked by "squeeze him in" and never let the phrase be used, making it the perfect choice as a code word of long standing. In this office it meant that the person in question was in disguise, something which happened often enough to require a code word. Just another day in Hollywood, except when you're expecting a visit from a certain stalker.

A speaker-box intercom had been the boss's choice over the simple and more private but lowly telephone, hence the code words among the staff. With her heart racing Jodie forced herself to speak up quickly and to use a reasonable tone of voice. "Uh, sure. In fact, I have a spare moment right now. Why don't you have Clarence bring us some tea?"

"Ms White, Clarence stepped out for a while."

"How long?"

"Just to the drug store." Dolly smiled up at the prospective client. He nodded knowingly. It was obvious to him that Ms White's assistant had gone on a drug buy, perfectly common in show biz. He was pleased to have one of his suspicions confirmed. However, it was not a valid euphemism for this office and as far as Jodie knew Dan had probably walked to the drug store down the block. "And didn't you tell Kevin you'd call him back at..." she glanced at the clock, her eyebrow raised on one side knowing it was extraordinarily absurd for her to say "...10:03? Should I have our guest come back at a more convenient time?" Oh, please, please, wished Dolly devoutly, let me tell him to come back later, tomorrow when I'm off!!

"No, no. I'm sure Clarence will be right back. Why don't you have him fill out the standard form and give me five minutes to call Kevin?" Jodie watched the lights to be sure she was disconnected then called the number in the little office which the boss had grudgingly allotted to the cops, the one with no windows and a 16 foot high ceiling. Bobby wasn't expected until 10:30 because of a prior court appearance. They'd barely started their surveillance. Had Dan left anyone else behind? No. The phone wasn't answered. They'd told her that the taping equipment was voice activated. Dan must have been confident of it or he wouldn't have left. She would have much preferred someone to be listening in, but she knew any evidence would be preserved regardless and she didn't want to give this guy time to be suspicious, if he was, in fact, Horace.

There was no Kevin for her to call and the waiting was getting to her. Completely unaware of what backup she had, at 10:10 she simply had to proceed. "You can send him in now."

The man who entered was indeed in disguise; a wig with no part, makeup that had smudged onto his collar. Dark rings around his eyes that gave him a vaguely east Indian look. She'd seen worse, so he wasn't a complete incompetent, and it beat the sunglasses and raincoat routine. The picture Dan had showed them all of Horace was a couple of years old. Horace had been unable to access his funds after his "death" so he'd had to start again from scratch. It seemed unlikely that he would have amassed enough money to get a surgical makeover. She stood to shake his hand and watched his face as he approached. This man was thinner, his eyes seemed to be more open. When he smiled there were fewer lines, but the dimples, hard to disguise the dimples. Jodie felt sure enough to proceed. She indicated that he should sit in the facing chair and made a point of not continuing to stare at him by restacking her papers. "Well, Mr...."

"Hancock."

"...Hancock, what did you want to see me about?"

He looked at Jodie only momentarily. His eyes studied the room, not a general sweep but a careful inventory, fixed on each item in the office in turn. The plants, the cleared off desktop, the window which was frosted over from the lime in the sprinkler water which hit it every night, the computer monitor, the phone. The wing back chair had been removed temporarily. The chair wasn't exceptionally comfortable, but it had been in her family and she liked the look of it. That's why she placed it so that she could see it. Moving it was a matter of tempting fate. If there was to be a shoot-out in her office the chair was sure to get it. Move the chair, deny the fate.

"Well, Ms White, I've written a screenplay which I believe has considerable potential. However, since I have not previously written for the screen I'm looking for an experienced screenwriter to help me with the subtle aspects of which I am ignorant."

"That's certainly a refreshing approach Mr. Hancock. Most new writers are carried away by their enthusiasm and assume that they know it all." She leaned back slightly in her chair and fingered a pen. Bobby had refused to tell her where the mikes had been placed so that she wouldn't unconsciously focus on them.

"Well, perhaps I'm a little older than most new writers." The barest mite of a doubt creeped into her considerations. It was a plausible story and his attitude was very self-deprecating. The man who'd called Hum seemed to lack finesse, he made demands, he let his anger speak.

"It's unusual but I suspect we could put you in touch with someone who could help you, IF it looks like your screenplay has any potential." '

"I understand. Certainly. And I would, of course, pay the writer for his time."

"Then if you would leave your screenplay at the front desk, we'll have it read and get back..." She hated risking his leaving, but there was no way an agent would follow any course other than to have the writer leave his script. To acquiesce to his request would have been so out of character as to scream 'WE'RE ONTO YOU!'

She was so intent on making her own performance plausible she almost missed it, but as she reached for papers he'd left on her desk she saw a look in his eyes that said quite clearly that he thought these people were stupid.

"Actually, I was hoping to be able to talk to a particular screenwriter." Okay, here it comes. God she hoped that the equipment was working. "I've seen a number of his works and been quite impressed with his versatility. So many people seem to confine themselves to one genre." He seemed to relax a little, warming up to the part. He must have spent days working out all the possible ways it could play, setting up contingencies in his script. He'd gotten his hearing, he'd seen the agent and she looked innocuous. He must have smelled a kind of victory.

Jodie treated him to a kindly smile; the poor deluded thing. "Mr. Hancock, as agents we act in behalf of our clients so that they are free to do what they do best. They don't meet with people until a lot of preliminary things..."

"Yes, I do understand, truly, but if I could just speak with him, I'm sure he'd agree to work with me."

Jodie shifted slightly in her chair. "Who did you have in mind, Mr. Hancock?"

"Humphrey Dixon."

YES!!! she screamed inside. "I see. And why did you come to me?" Jodie's tone was of serious inquiry.

"Come now, Ms White, you are his agent."

Jodie knew the look she was giving him. She'd practiced in front of a mirror in high school prior to an eventful encounter with a guy who'd informed everyone that he was going to nail Jodie on their next date. Her I-don't-know-what-you're-talking-about look was perfection. "That's not commonly known, Mr. Hancock."

"Perhaps not among the general public but within the business all references to Humphrey Dixon lead to you." He smiled like a cat who knows a shortcut to the mouse hole.

"So you have connections in the business?"

"I have a friend who has a friend..." This was going way too good. What else should she try to get out of him? Was the mere fact that he was looking for Humphrey enough for Dan? Quickly Jodie signaled the front desk.

"Dolly, what about that tea, has Clarence come back yet?" If she offered up Humphrey as a prize, it might draw him in and make him tip his hand. However, it was just as likely that he would be expecting much more opposition after Humphrey and the agency had gone to such trouble to hide.

"Yes, he's getting it right now."

"Good. Well, Mr. Hancock, I'm afraid that Mr. Dixon is one writer I won't be able to put you in touch with even if we were inclined to make that sort of connection."

"Yes, I'm aware that he's out of town, but all I need is to talk to him. If I could just have his number..."

"Now, how would you know that he's out of town?" she asked in her best imitation of Lea Thompson.

"His answering service. I wouldn't have bothered you if I'd been able to get hold of him directly."

"How long have you been looking for Mr. Dixon?"

"Just a few weeks. He seems to have been gone for longer than the usual vacation, so I assumed he was away working, perhaps on location."

She nodded a noncommittal nod which could have been empathy or a confirmation of his guess. "So, you know Humphrey's work? Did you happen to see his last picture, "Wreckage"?"

He tensed up noticeably. "It was very imaginative." Jodie just stared at him. "Such a thing could never happen, of course, but it certainly made for a thrilling chase."

"Oh, it seemed to me that the plot was quite plausible." Jodie's eyes opened wide as Dan walked in carefully balancing a tray loaded with tea things. His hair was wet and slicked straight back. Jacketless, his shirt was fetchingly opened three buttons down. His movements were quick and birdlike. Jodie realized he was trying to appear gay and suppressed a grin. "I wouldn't have thought of it myself but I can envision someone taking advantage of such a situation." Dan made like the caring host, his fluttering clearly demonstrating subordinance. Jodie was greatly comforted by his presence but feigned annoyance at his puttering.

"As I said, I didn't find the plot believable."

"Yet, you want to work with him. Curious. Tell me, Mr. Hancock, what exactly did you find farfetched? Did you think that the man wouldn't have wanted revenge?"

"No, I suspect he would have. But that's immater..."

"Or perhaps that he wouldn't have been able to establish a new identity?"

"I suspect that is harder than most people would think, but..."

"Or that he wouldn't have been satisfied stopping with those enemies he did get? Maybe he would come to see that there were others who might be able to expose him?" Jodie was smiling amiably, the picture of a devoted agent seeking an opinion that might pertain to her client. Her target halted all movement and looked at her intently. His eyes squinted just a little but that didn't help him see any better.

"No, I think he went quite far enough."

"I'm sorry Mr. Hancock, how did you say you got Mr. Dixon's number?" Dan was still puttering, trying to look like he should stay without overtly taking part in the conversation. 'God,' he thought, 'she's good with that innocent look.'

"Oh, just a friend. No big deal."

"Same friend who said I was his agent?"

"Wasn't there a break in at Universal a while back? Their files would have had Humphrey's agent listed." Dan offered innocently as he busied himself with the remaining tea things.

"Now, listen, I didn't break in anywhere. I got the number from a friend who's good at finding things."

"Who would that be, maybe it's the guy we use?" Jodie looked instantly intrigued.

"I really don't think that's important." There was still nothing in his look to show that he suspected her of any duplicity. It seemed more likely that he thought she was a flake, a flake he wouldn't get any information out of.

"No, but it might be useful to us at some point. Being in the right place, knowing the right people. That's what it's all about, you know, location, location, location." She was just about as chipper as she'd ever been. "Which brings me back to Humphrey. Since he's in a different location, I'm afraid we can't grant your request. We can still look at your script and maybe set you up with a different coach."

"No, I'm afraid it has to be Mr. Dixon. See, besides needing his expertise, which is considerable," he nodded to her respectfully, "there's another reason I want to get in touch with him, and only him. We were good friends back in high school, I'd like to surprise him."

"Oooo," Jodie squealed and startled Dan so that he rattled the tray, "so you went to school in Long Beach too. How exciting! He tells me he was short as a child and only grew tall when he started having sex. Is that true?"

"Well, I can't vouch for when he started having sex, but he was a short kid, kind of a nerd, really, we were both of us kind of outcasts." He had perked up, encouraged by this newfound enthusiasm. He smelled success.

"You know maybe just this once..." Jodie stared off into imagination.

"Uh, Ms White, I thought Mr. Dixon played basketball in high school." Dan stood near the door. When Horace turned toward him Dan touched his finger to his chin and looked toward the ceiling.

"Why you're absolutely right Clarence. For an old friend I might have been able to make some arrangement, but it must be a different Humphrey Dixon that you went to high school with."

"No, no, really. It's him. I swear. He lives on 10th, drives a Mazda convertible."

"Why, yes, yes he does. Now, isn't that interesting? I'm curious Mr. Hancock, if you know where he lives and what his car is you must have been there, why didn't you just talk to him then?"

"He wasn't home. He must have already left for...where did you say he'd gone?"

"He's off doing research. I'm afraid my contact with him is spotty. Maybe I can have him call you?"

"No, I'd rather surprise him." Everything about him became quiet, like he'd been shuttled off onto a sidetrack and had to shut down until he could get back on track. Dan recognized the posture and gave Jodie a nod. The chair creaked a little as Horace rose to leave.

"Don't you find that interesting, Clarence? Here our Humphrey Dixon grew up in Santa Barbara and yet Mr. Evans here knew him from high school in Long Beach. That's a heck of a commute. They must have had a really good chess club."

He stared at Dan who was blocking the door. "Hancock. It's Hancock."

"Fine with me Mr. Hancock. You have the right to remain..." Jodie didn't hear the rest as Dan handcuffed Horace Evans and walked him out the door where he was met by Bobby, who looked in at Jodie with the biggest grin she'd ever seen on a cop.

Chapter 39

Tuesday night there was a small piece in the paper about a man named Humphrey Dixon who had been identified around town as Mason Landers. This had been reported to the police by Janice Renault. Anyone who knew how to contact Mr. Landers was asked to get in touch with the police.

Chapter 40

"So, what can you tell me about the case? I'm assuming you brought me out here so that we wouldn't be overheard."

"I told you she was a smart lady, Dan." Bobby had insisted that they find the time to fill Jodie in on the progress of the case after the help she'd provided them. This was not standard procedure but Dan figured they needed to eat anyway. A walk along one of the local tourist centers with a little take-out was about as inconspicuous as one could get. "Horace refused to talk. You recall that he didn't say another word in your office."

"Yeah, he clammed right up." Bobby noticed how Jodie's simple cotton dress molded to her body by the breeze they faced. Maybe it was being away from the office, maybe it was the pressure being off, but she seemed to almost skip along, carefree and playful.

"Apparently our Horace isn't completely back on his feet yet. Couldn't afford an attorney. Wouldn't dare turn to any former associates. An attorney was appointed for him, but he still refused to talk."

Dan took over while Bobby chewed. "We kind of expected he might have IDs for the Hancock identity but he was just winging that one. All his cards were for John Regland. The real John Regland died in Idaho as a kid back in the seventies. Our Horace was working as a respected employee of a large trucking company. Worked his way up from dispatcher to a management job in less than a year. Has a pretty wife who's screaming mistaken identity."

Jodie nodded. "It would be quite a shock to find out your husband had a vicious past. On the other hand, you wouldn't expect her to react any other way even if she did know."

"Right. You know, that was an interesting point you got out of him, where he'd found your name. We were able to get his phone records and have been tracking down all the numbers. Allowing that some of the calls were made by the wife there's a call to an area TV station that looks promising. Neither one of them can explain it and the station can't tell who the call was transferred to."

Jodie stopped strolling. They stopped as well and faced her. She squinted up at Bobby. "That's rather interesting. Humphrey, where he's hiding, has been followed by a woman who we think is a weather girl at KFIV."

The guys exchanged looks. "That's the station!"

"What do you mean he's being followed? Why didn't you tell us?"

"That could have a bearing on our case."

"No. No. See she isn't after Humphrey, she's after Mason, the guy Hum is posing as." The cops shared another glance, less surprise, more incredulity. "Sorry. Hum has an old friend who lives in this little town. Hum went to stay there and decided to let everybody think he was really his friend. Because he didn't really know anyone there and Humphrey thought it would be safer. I thought it was a pretty dumb idea, but by the time I heard about it he'd already started it so what could I do?" The cops responded with shifting eyebrows. "Yeah, I know how it sounds... trust me, everybody there thought he was his friend including this Cicily Trimble. She's been asking about him all over town."

"But she doesn't know he's Humphrey?"

"She didn't. He was just found out the other day."

"By her?"

"No. It was a local librarian. He was taken in by the cops." They nodded. Those cops probably asked for info from someone in the area. Probably Santa Monica. They'd look into it.

"Why was he taken in?"

"Well," Jodie replied with great irony hoping to minimize rousing their suspicions, "Apparently this librarian figured out he wasn't his friend and made a Butch and Sundance leap to the conclusion that he'd killed him. His friend. Which, of course he didn't." When she looked at them she didn't like the skepticism in their eyes. What had she left out? "Oh, they let him out. They still want to hear from Mason, but Humphrey doesn't know where he is so... Well, I'm sure it will all work its way out."

"So you don't think this weather girl was working with Horace?"

"Nope. She was definitely looking for information about Mason."

"Why?"

"Something about blowing the whistle, industrial espionage, whatever." This gave them a new wrinkle in the case which they didn't want to see. But she was probably right and it was a beautiful day for a walk, why dwell on it?

"So, Ms White, what do you think Dan's chances are in show biz? Sounded to me like he made a fairly convincing alternative lifestyle advocate." Jodie laughed.

"He was very good. Certainly had Horace fooled. Have you done this kind of thing often, Dan?"

"Sure, regularly." He shook his head at the thought of the reputation he might get from this. "Actually, I did some undercover work which amounts to acting. Kind of miss it. Somewhere else a guy like me could probably do some community theatre, but here, look who you have to compete with? I'll stick to what I do best."

"Okay, but if you ever need an agent…"

Chapter 41

Humphrey recovered from his malaise enough to become ambulatory. He was stuck on low maintenance however, reduced to staring at the TV, going to the bathroom, sleeping wherever he happened to be. He hadn't been at such a loss since when his first movie deal fell through leaving him with $4000 in bills he'd run up in anticipation. He'd learned from that.

Mid-afternoon he heard a bell, somewhere. It finally registered as a phone but it wasn't the one next to him. Mechanically he rose and followed the sound. His cell phone was in the pocket of his coat in the closet. "Yeah?"

"Hum, you okay?"

"Jodie?"

"Yes. What's wrong, you sound half dead?"

"Close." He waited until he'd reclaimed his place in the recliner. "Things were going real well. That day I spent at the flower shop? That was great. Then Bryna loaded up my files to see if they'd saved okay and she started reading them. I was such an idiot to ask her to check the files. She figured out right off what they were and told Orinda, who threw me out."

"So you're back at Mason's?"

"Yeah. I tried to tell them it would all come out different but they didn't want to listen. I'm hoping that if I give them enough time they'll hear me out. This is all your fault for telling Bryna I used people as characters."

"You do. And how can it be all my fault when you're the one who screwed up?"

"Things were clicking along. All that work. It was all falling into place. They'll never let me use it now. If I try, they'll sue."

"Maybe this will cheer you up. We had our sting."

"Oh, yeah, I forgot. Sorry."

"'Sokay, you've been preoccupied. Dan and Bobby came to monitor the bugs and, like, first thing, this guy comes with a script and a disguise." It still made her laugh to think about the wig and all. "I let him in and talked to him and I was playing him along, you know, afraid he wasn't the guy, when he said what he really wanted was to talk to Humphrey Dixon to get help on his script.

"I thought I'd suffocate I was so shocked and excited. I humored him…"

Things were starting to sink in. "Uh, wait. I thought you were going to have someone stand in for you."

"Yeah, we talked about doing that but I decided it would work better…"

"Jodie! You promised me you wouldn't play around with your safety."

"I know, Hum, but I gave it a lot of thought and I just had to do it myself."

"Why?"

"Lots of reasons. Disruption of routine, believable performance…"

"Performance?" He imagined a Jodie dressed inexplicably in a figure skater's costume, front and center at the Hollywood Bowl accepting the adulation of thousands.

"We needed to get him to say something implicating himself. If he didn't get the responses he expected he would have walked."

"And the cops would have followed."

"Yeah, but they wouldn't have had the evidence. Hum this was really important. I did this for you, to get this guy off the streets as soon as possible."

"For me? Un huh. Jodie, what's in this for you?"

Dang, he'd nabbed her. A solid curtain of wounded innocence was in order. "Humphrey?"

"Ah, you want to be part of the story, don't you? You want writing credits."

"Humphrey, I'm shocked that you would think…" She couldn't go on and still keep the laugh out of her voice. "So, you want to hear what happened?"

"Yes."

"We got him to admit that he'd been watching you, that he knew you were out of town. Turns out he's been to your house, knew what car you drove."

"Shit."

"It wasn't exactly a confession but it was enough to take him in where they can prove that he's Horace Evans and get him on the murders even if they don't have enough on the stalking. And get this, I got him to talk about how he'd found me and he implicated someone at the same TV station as Cicily Trimble."

Hum was almost completely revived by that. "Really? Do you think they're connected?"

"We'll find out, but, remember, you were sure she was looking for Mason."

"Yeah, everything pointed to that. All the things she accused me of at the drug store had to do with whatever she thought Mason was up to. Weird.

"So he's in custody?"

"Yeah. You can come home now free of fear."

"It wasn't fear that brought me here, it was my agent bugging me about getting some work done. Of course, now that's a bust. Anyway, I still can't leave town until they decide about Mase."

"Hum?"

"No. I am not calling him."

"Okay, okay. I just wanted you to know how it went."

"Isn't today Wednesday? I thought it was set for Tuesday."

"It was. I didn't want to get your hopes up until I heard from Bobby about how strong the case was, you know, in case they had to let him go."

"Let him go. Yeah, you were right. That would have made my day."

Chapter 42

For three days Humphrey had been essentially confined to unmonitored house arrest. He didn't want to encounter Cicily anymore and anticipated no enjoyment from his usually activities. He had finally figured out what fuse controlled the doorbell so that he wouldn't have to hear it and had figured out that if he crawled from the living room to the hall he couldn't be seen by the average height person lurking at the door. He'd tested this late Monday night by going out and peering through the little window while affecting different heights. This was the high point of his day and only accomplishment.

On Tuesday Ace came by with an officer. Humphrey rolled his eyes when he answered the door to their hail. This didn't impress the cops.

"Mr. Dixon, we've looked over your computer."

Humphrey turned around and returned to the recliner leaving the cops to come in and shut the door. "It's Mason's computer."

"Indeed. Curious thing about the files on this computer. There's one of them that's been saved over and over under different names. How do you explain that?"

"I don't know. I never bothered looking at Mason's files. I figured they were private." A slight rise of his eyebrows served to implicate them.

"Un huh. And there's nothing that's been added since you came." He stood as close as he could between Humphrey and the TV, notebook in hand. It was unclear whether he was consulting his notes or preparing to capture Humphrey's heartfelt if delayed confession.

"That would be because I saved everything to floppies, sent them off to my agent."

"So you have a backup copy on floppy?"

"No. Stupid of me, but then it looks like I've been pretty stupid about this whole affair, doesn't it?"

Ace stared at him and smirked. Too easy. "No printouts?"

"No. Sorry. I run off a few sheets now and then but I never save them." He consoled himself that truth half the time showed an effort.

"Okay, we've got your computer out in the car."

The officer turned to go get it while Humphrey mumbled, "Mason's computer."

"Well, if Mr. Landers ever gets back I'm sure he'll appreciate that you preserved his privacy and good name."

Hum nodded while maintaining his view of the TV screen as if that commercial were his ticket out. "You don't sound very convincing Mr. Bennett. You might want to consider an acting class."

"Everything's make believe where you come from, isn't it?"

Hum adopted a silly grin which melted instantly to sullen. "We try."

The police left having deposited the computer on the living room floor. After ignoring it for half an hour Humphrey got a screwdriver from the kitchen drawer and opened up as many parts as he could figure out. The cops he had worked with in his research would have planted a bug just in case things didn't work out. He didn't find anything that looked like it shouldn't be there, but, he realized, how would he know? There were suspicious looking lintel-like pieces but they looked to be welded in place and part of a circuit. There were beads that reminded him of the tubes his grandpa used to replace in that old TV. There were things that fell out that he wasn't sure if he got them back the same way as similar pieces. He took it back to the basement and, after a little difficulty putting it back together, set it up.

From the hidden floppy he looked over the files that he thought he remembered seeing Bryna open just to get an idea of what they had against him. It wasn't good. He was reluctant to continue working on the script because he felt sure, in their present state of animosity, the Waters women would hamper his efforts to sell a completed script. But he needed to keep busy, having already watched all the videos Mason had on hand several times over, so he thought he better write up his recollections of the recent events. He wanted to get the reality down before he turned it into anything else.

He found comfort in being busy after whole days of TV. By Thursday he'd filled in all the particulars and turned back to his working script. It was good. Reading through it again after an absence it seemed to be better than he'd thought before. But the storyboards in his head were not the by now familiar scenes of the story he was constructing, but himself watching from behind an oval mirror (quite like the one in Snow White), watching himself read the story oblivious to the mirror image begging to be heard.

Humphrey pushed it from his mind and tried to bring back the useful images: the lucky florist, the con man, the duped neighbors. But the Free in the mirror was stronger than any trapped fairy tale wizard and Hum couldn't keep from seeing himself reading: from behind the mirror, from the toe of his shoe, from the spider on the ceiling, from the remains of the sandwich on the counter. Thoroughly frustrated, Hum stepped away from the computer, trudged up the stairs and gazed out over the sparkling snow, thinking that if his mind was intent on wandering off on its own, he might as well have something both soothing and attractive to occupy his barely conscious self. Some time after the setting sun robbed him of the snow sparkles, Humphrey blinked himself awake and got back to satisfying his basic needs.

Chapter 43

On Wednesday a longer article appeared in the paper:

> It was reported Tuesday that Humphrey Dixon had been questioned about using the identity of local resident Mason Landers. Dixon has indicated that he came to Brookings because someone was stalking him in his native Los Angeles. On Tuesday an arrest was made in that case. The suspect is also under investigation in a number of murders. Dixon, the writer of the movie "Wreckage" which is scheduled to open in town Friday, was presumably targeted by the suspect because he, like the movie character, had allegedly faked his death in a ferry wreck and returned to seek revenge.
>
> Landers, who has not been in Brookings for several months, has been under investigation by Cicily Trimble, from KFIV TV in Los Angeles. Trimble is on leave from her job as weather announcer and was unaware that Dixon was posing as Landers. Trimble contends that Landers is involved in industrial cover-ups. Landers could not be reached.
>
> Janice Renault, who alerted the police of Dixon's false identity, was unaware of Dixon's true identity and made the report because she feared for Landers' life. Dixon and Landers were said to have been college roommates. Dixon, who was unavailable for comment, will remain in Brookings, possibly continuing research on his next project, until Landers can be contacted.

Janice had been gratified by the mention of her name in the Tuesday paper. She worked Wednesday evenings and was looking forward to seeing if there was a follow-up. She'd heard on Tuesday that Dixon had been released and a call to the chief had assured her that he wasn't off the hook.

She'd noticed a few people looking at her more than casually while she performed her duties, but she'd assumed admiration was behind their interest. She would smile at them and nod magnanimously in appreciation of their attentions and think about how humiliating it must be for Bryna.

Then she got home and read the paper. "Killer? He's famous? Weather announcer? She's not even a reporter? Roommate? Damn."

Bryna was shown the article when the paper arrived at the library in late afternoon. When they checked the paper in they always looked for things like coupons and mentions of the library. The coupons get marked 'void' so that people won't cut them out. She was careful not to show much of a reaction to those who were watching her read, but inside she was beaming with vindication. Why hadn't he just told her about the stalker? "Interesting," was all she would say.

Humphrey had not subscribed to the paper. He'd not seen the first mention on Tuesday but he'd suspected something was about to be printed when he checked in with the police and Mike told him the paper had been asking about him. There had been phone calls he hadn't answered and knocks at the door he'd ignored. So he drove out late at night to pick up a copy at the gas station.

Cicily, who had read the paper when she first got to town and found it trivial, hadn't seen the Tuesday notice. In her booth when she went to Perkins for dinner was a Wednesday issue left by the previous customer. She picked it up merely as a diversion while waiting for her omelet. She'd felt the blood drain from her head as she read the augmented version. She read it again and again. She was numb when the waitress brought her plate. Finding her unresponsive the waitress had tapped her shoulder, thinking the worst and searching her memory for the steps to take should CPR or the Heimlich be needed. Cicily came to enough to wave her away.

How had they found out all of that? Who's Janice? How did they know who she was? They must have talked to someone at KFIV. Great, the manager would be real impressed now.

The waitress was surprised when she returned with her check that the customer hadn't touched anything, hadn't moved. Cicily stared at her for quite some time. Looking at the food made her nauseous. As if she were suddenly out of time she gathered her things and started out the door. They called after her, caught her in the parking lot. Reluctantly she focused enough to dig in her bag and throw them a ten. It took her one minute to get to her room, two to throw her things in a bag and five minutes to check out. She had no idea when the next flight out was, but she was determined not to wait for it in Brookings.

An hour later she realized that taking the next flight out, to O'Hare, would cost her an extra $400 which she wouldn't be able to recoup from her never-to-be new job as reporter. So she checked into an airport motel and called Harlon.

"You jerk. This is all your fault."

"Nice to hear your voice too, Cicily."

"Why didn't you get me a photo of this Landers? There must have been some DMV record for him somewhere. I've been following the wrong guy!!!"

"No shit?"

She was pacing the three feet available to her by the motel phone, waving her free hand around like a trapped bird. "And it gets better. The guy I was following was hiding out here from LA where he was being stalked by a serial killer. I just missed out on the scoop of a lifetime and it's your fault!"

"Why is it my fault?"

"Because intelligence was your department."

She imagined Harlon leaning back and casually filing his nails, not only oblivious to her torment but relishing in it. "For which I was never paid."

"And never will be!"

"Anyway, I haven't heard about any serial killer or anybody being stalked."

"Watch for it. The victim is Humphrey Dixon and he's a screenwriter."

"Shit!"

"What? What?" Her first 'what' was filled with loud belligerence, the second was tinged with concern, intrigue, hope.

"Uh, nothing. Nothing at all. Look Cicily I'm sorry you spent so much time on this guy. I've been getting better info lately out of the cleanup lead. I think you should check out the guy in El Paso."

"Oh forget it. You think there's a chance in hell the station isn't going to laugh me out of town?"

"Maybe they won't find out about it."

"Someone knew I was the weather girl. They must have called the station. They've got to know already."

"So, you coming back?"

"Yeah. I have had enough of South Dakota." Besides, she'd left many of her new clothes in the room back in Brookings. That had been the plan all along, but now it occurred to her that she might not be working in LA after all.

Chapter 44

Janice slept fitfully and came to work looking like an angry, resentful, well made-up professional. She considered calling in sick but there was a videoconference meeting scheduled which she felt was important for her, to establish her credentials among area librarians. She chose to forego break when she noticed people whispering in the hall. Most people read the signs and stayed away. Geri's curiosity was too keen to let a little animosity deter her.

"Janice, what gives with this Landers guy?"

"Need I remind you that just because this Dixon is hiding from a killer doesn't mean he can't be a killer himself. In fact, it would be the perfect cover."

"But there's no body."

"Not yet. Who knows where the crime might have taken place?"

Geri turned and left, mumbling as she went, "No arguing with that."

Janice decided to go to the videoconference studio early to get away from the eyes she felt upon her. Bad move. Bryna and another librarian also arrived early and Janice had no choice but to stay.

"So what's this thing in the paper all about?" asked the other librarian, Zeta.

Janice thought that if it were anyone but Zeta she might be able to ignore her as though she hadn't been heard, but Zeta had taken an assertiveness course which had transformed her life. Janice finally spoke, with deliberation, as though the words each had to pass an evaluation before being uttered. She clung to the papers she'd brought, studying them with fierce desperation. "I saw a situation which was unusual. I felt it was necessary to alert someone of the potential…ramifications so that it could be properly investigated."

"I heard you'd talked to this weather person about her investigations. That would have been some report. 'Tune in at 10 folks for word about a severe hunk front stalled in the area. Could be a killer.'" Zeta laughed with abandon. Janice gave a mighty sigh, for at that moment she noticed that four more had arrived for the meeting, remaining quiet as they found seats, apparently hoping to catch the rest of the discussion. "So she didn't know she was following the wrong guy. But you knew. Curious you didn't tell her. Almost like you wanted her to look like a fool. Funny how that worked out." Had she not been focused on her papers she might have seen the aborted smiles.

Arron had only moments before been filled in on the news item. He hadn't had time to fully appreciate the level of ridicule to which Janice could expect to be subjected. "Sometimes it's better to go out on a limb, if you might be sorry later for not having acted."

Zeta countered, "That's true, Arron, but the guy was a respected big-time screenwriter. He'd done nothing suspicious. From what I hear people liked him." Janice so wanted to point out that Bryna hadn't known who he really was either, no one had. Not knowing who he really wasn't her fault. At least she knew who he wasn't. No one else had figured that out. Why was no one seeing that crucial point? "Just because you know everyone in town doesn't mean you shouldn't trust strangers. You know what he's going to do now, don't you? You can bet on it. Now that they've found this guy who was after him, he's going to write this up as a movie. You might even get to play yourself Janice." There were a dozen people at the meeting now and it was time to start. Janice was grateful for the diversion which served to delay her realizing what the presence of those people meant. They were people from all over the area, people who would take back with them their image of the defining moment when Zeta forced Janice to see the extent of what was in store for her.

Bryna said nothing. She only shrugged when someone asked her something, something they didn't pursue because everyone was listening in on Zeta and Janice. She had not been mentioned in the article although she knew she was part of the story that was slowly circulating. Bryna found herself wishing that Humphrey could have been here to see this. It was the payback her mother had assured him would happen without his intervention. Yes, he probably would write it up and they would all be part of it. And making sure he told it right, dang if that didn't sound like a reasonable price to pay. She made a note at the top of her page to call Mom.

Janice happened to see Bryna smiling. She was smiling at the prospects of ending the fight with Humphrey though she could as easily have been smiling at something said in the conference. But Janice didn't notice the others smiling as well, so it was unlikely that she would ever let Bryna off her shit list.

Chapter 45

The house phone rang. During his time in the house Humphrey had often ignored it since it turned out to be primarily telemarketers. Since his "arrest" he'd decided to answer in machine mode so that he could screen the calls. If it were Bryna or Orinda willing to talk to him again he didn't want to miss the opportunity, or maybe the cops would relent. So far it had mainly been the press or the boldly curious. "At the tone, say your piece, beep."

"Humphrey?"

He turned quickly, ramming his hand into the side of the refrigerator. The glass that the hand held bounced across the floor, the cold Pepsi seeped into his socks. "Bryna? Don't hang up!"

After a pause that made him worry that she had hung up she replied tolerantly, "Humphrey, I called you."

"Ah, yeah, okay. Just hear me out." He hated sounding so desperate but he knew timing was everything, except for location, and preparation, and attitude.

"Humphrey, do you know anything about me? Do you know what I eat, my favorite color, my aspirations, where I like to vacation, what I have hidden in a box in the back of my closet?"

This was not what he expected. It felt like a trap. "No."

"No. But you trusted me anyway, didn't you?"

"Yeah."

"Any idea why?"

He'd been wiping up his spill, the task being compounded by the wet socks that spread the sticky area farther as he walked around. He stopped to ponder. He thought he probably was supposed to know the answer to her question but if he said he did she was sure to ask him to explain so once again truth won out. "No."

"No. But I came through for you didn't I?" He nodded. "And you'd be the first to say I knew nothing about you, yet I told you things no one else had, I defied the police for you, I trusted you with my mother."

"Yes, you did."

"Do you know why?"

There it was again. Better embellish. "No, but I'm grateful."

Bryna sounded impressed, he felt sure she was grinning. "Contrite, nice choice. Listen, Humphrey, you took the disk with you but several of your files were already opened. Considering the circumstances it seemed judicious for us to read them. Mother was quite upset at finding how she's been portrayed...."

"Bryna, you've got..."

"Eh, eh, eh. Learn when to sit tight."

"I'm tight."

"...but I was able to point out to her, after careful reading, that there were references to changes to be made in the character."

"Yes! Yes! That's what I've been trying to say. She was just a starting point. Before I'm done she won't recognize herself in that character at all."

"Mother and I talked about this for some time. We decided on a solution but things have changed."

"What's changed?"

"I was at a meeting this morning with Janice."

Humphrey shuddered. He hoped he'd never have to meet her again. "Gloating is she?"

"No. As a matter of fact she's quite miserable."

Humphrey was instantly revived. "Really?"

"Humphrey, that's a rather evil tone in your voice." She was glad to hear him perking up. He was as glad to have Bryna teasing him as he was to imagine Janice being miserable. "Why don't you meet me at Mother's and I'll tell you all about it."

He looked around at the sodden socks on the floor, at the brown drips on the side of the fridge, at the piles of dirty dishes he'd been avoiding. They could all wait. "Is Orinda willing to see me? She was pretty mad when I left."

"Do you think I would invite you to an ambush? She's quite eager to put this matter behind us."

"You're not going to throw me around again are you?"

"No." Not unless you want me to, she thought. "That was purely a defensive measure. If you behave yourself it won't be necessary for me to mop the floor with you. Can you come now?"

He was fairly sure she couldn't take him in a fair fight but thought better of saying so. She might just want to take him up on it. "On my way."

Humphrey was wary as he waited at the door. Bryna was smiling when she opened it and what he was hit with was the smell of chocolate chip cookies. Orinda was lifting cookies off a sheet and the kitchen table held three large glasses of milk and a banana. Orinda acknowledged him but didn't say anything. Bryna threw his coat on a chair and proceeded to describe for them the videoconference meeting, embellishing the tale with background information on the other participants. They were all seated around the table digging into the cookies, still gooey from the oven. Humphrey watched Orinda and only laughed when she laughed but didn't relax until Bryna got to the part about Humphrey writing it up as a movie.

Orinda squealed with delight and reached over to shove Humphrey in the shoulder. She sat there grinning at him like it had all been part of her plan. "After that article her only hope was that people would soon forget. That won't happen now. People at the meeting will go home and talk. Colleagues all over the state will hear about it. If you write this up as a screenplay, at the very least you'll have to talk to people here and dredge it all up again, at most it would be produced and everyone in the state will know it is Janice no matter how much you change the character."

Humphrey shook his head as if bothered by a gnat. "Wait a minute, you want me to write this up?"

"Why not?" Orinda wiped a chocolate drip from her chin.

"But the story about the shop…"

"The story, as good as it does seem to be from what we saw, points directly at Orinda and much of it is pure fantasy. This is quite different."

"But the flower shop character is a good person."

"Indeed. But that isn't the problem, Free. Bryna and I talked about it extensively and decided to allow you to continue if you changed the shop from flowers to something else. I know you've done all this research, but there are too many people in town who know of your association with me." While Orinda spoke, Humphrey was being distracted by Bryna. She had first carefully selected two cookies of equal size and shape. Then she started peeling the banana and cut half-inch thick slices which she arranged on the underside of one cookie. When done she placed the other cookie on top and held it poised for a bite.

"If you make the character less than Orinda actually is, people will assume you've discovered the real Orinda Waters and disregard their own experiences. If you change the character the way you planned to, she can't do flowers." She bit into the sandwich carefully so that it wouldn't shatter, a technique apparently based on years of practice. Savoring the tastes and textures and temperatures her eyes half closed in a wave of rapture.

Humphrey was most intrigued by this pageant. Reluctantly he refocused. "Are you saying you want me to make the character more like your mother?"

"Mmm. That would be fine with me but she thinks that if everyone sees that it's her they'll also think that she won the money. And...she didn't."

"But then it's a completely different story."

"And maybe you really did know about this guy on the ferry."

He pouted. Given the difficult line of reasoning they were throwing at him, they found it endearing. "You're saying that I'll be forgiven if I make it say, a shoe store or a card shop? But there isn't the same passion with cards or shoes that you get with flowers. People don't dream of retiring and opening a shoe store."

"What about books?" Orinda had finished her milk which apparently marked the end of her cookie quota. She sat with her arms folded on the table enjoying the game.

"Hmm. Books. Yeah. Passion, no profit, competition. Might work."

"Good. We want you to look into how the changes would work out. We can help you with it if you'd like. However, those changes are now secondary to our main...demand." Bryna popped the last piece of cookie sandwich in her mouth and licked her fingers. Humphrey looked from one to the other with a building dread. "We're assuming that Zeta was right about your writing this up."

"The probability is high. If Jodie has anything to say about it."

"Good. We want to be involved."

"Involved?"

"We realize that the story is much bigger than our part in it, but we feel it is important that our part be subject to our input."

Hum frowned. "You want to help write it?"

Bryna looked to her mother. Orinda looked over at a Humphrey who looked as though he were finally realizing she held the last ace. "We wouldn't presume to second-guess your writing talents, Free. We just want to be sure things are treated judiciously. I'm sure it will come down to some legal agreement, but basically, if we don't have a say in how Brookings is handled we'll fight you on the lottery winner story."

"Orinda, I don't want to fight you on anything..." The phone rang. Orinda went to get it. Bryna finished her milk with a smack of complete satisfaction. Hum reached over and wiped the corner of her mouth with his finger. When Orinda returned she handed him the receiver. "Free, it's Steve, the city attorney."

"Have you got speaker phone on this?"

"Sure, if you want." She went back and touched the proper button.

He turned to Bryna and said, "I'd like some witnesses on this, whatever it is. Yes?"

"Mr. Dixon. I just had a call from Senate minority leader Daschle. They had me call him back just so that I would be sure it was legit. He has been notified by the director of the EPA that the man we've been looking for, Mason Landers, is indeed alive and well but unable to come and verify that fact. I must assume that he's in a jungle, on a sub or undercover. In any case that closes our investigation and you are free to go, if you so wish."

"Ha! Thank you. Thank you very much."

"You're welcome. Say goodbye to Orinda for me, will you?"

They were silent until Orinda pushed the button again, then all three erupted in leaps of joy. "Complete vindication. Is this the perfect ending to your story or what?" Bryna threw herself into his arms and they danced around the confines of the kitchen.

"But how do we let everybody know? Or..." he stopped dead, "...maybe it's better not to let them know."

"Oh, you want Janice to know for sure. I'll bet you anything she's still telling people that just because you're here legitimately doesn't mean you didn't already kill Mason."

Orinda sat again, quite self-satisfied. "Oh, the word will get out, you can be sure. If we don't see something in the paper by tomorrow, we'll drop a strategic hint to Kasey."

"Who's Kasey?"

"The reporter who broke the story. Seems she ran into Cicily when she was still trying to find you after your jail time and got her to admit a few things."

Suddenly his face went blank. "How did the head of the EPA know to call this senator?"

"Uh, me." He glared at Bryna. "I copied down the numbers from your phone bills before I hid them and figured out which number you'd called to get Mason. I left a message about your situation."

"Bryna!! I specifically told you I didn't want Mason bothered."

She shrugged. "I did it before I saw you at the station. I figured a little message wouldn't hurt. If he was as good a friend as it seemed, he would want to know even if there was nothing he could do. I talked to a woman who said she couldn't verify anything, so I had no idea if the message ever got to him. I guess it did." She grinned sheepishly but with no real regret.

Humphrey could only manage to shake his head. Bryna offered him another cookie which he took without thinking.

Chapter 46

Bryna was at the desk and saw him as he walked in. He was wearing the clothes he'd arrived in back in January having not worn them since. She acknowledged the difference with a head to toe gaze and half smile. "I have to be leaving soon."

"I see that you'll be going back to lovely weather." She'd offered to drive him down to Sioux Falls, but he'd already made arrangements and, tempting as it was, didn't want to take her away from her work. He needed to remain in the good graces of the administration if his work was going to proceed as he expected.

"It often is. You should come out and see for yourself. I'd look forward to showing you around." He smiled and continued watching her. Finally she shook her head and stared at her feet. If she waited much longer, she was likely to blush. "Given the circumstances we really didn't get to know each other. I mean, I wasn't really me, most of the time."

"Oh, so it's really Mason who's so charming, kind and clever. Lucky for me he still lives here."

He'd walked into that one. "Actually he is a good guy. But you've got to consider that he isn't around much. And he doesn't go out much when he is here and he's very serious." He leaned in closer to whisper, "And apparently he works for the government." He lingered close longer than he needed to and she let him. She still wondered why he smelled of cinnamon.

"And he's really the one who's a klutz and who gets too busy to get a haircut. How thorough of you to have adopted those traits for your simulation," she proclaimed facetiously.

"Yeah, well, you weren't always what you seemed either." Her eyebrows raised and her spine straightened a little. "You could have mentioned Orinda and all your inside information. I never knew librarians could be so sneaky."

"Yes. You have a lot to learn. But there's still time. I understand you have plenty of work to do once you get home. Jodie thinks you'll want to get to this story before you finish what you were working on."

"Jodie can be delusional. And when did you talk to her?"

"I called her. To make sure she knew you were free and coming home. She seems to be quite devoted to you. I think she must care for you more than you know. You're not just a source of income."

Humphrey thought on that. "Perhaps." Things had slowed down a bit and Bryna sensed that her staff was being a little too attentive to her conversation. She moved toward the door, he followed.

"When you do get around to writing this up, you're going to call, aren't you?"

Humphrey smiled. "That was the deal. Do you want it in writing?"

"Writing between friends? Humphrey, after all we've been through? You can fax it to me." She grinned big and he had to laugh. He kissed her cheek and she leaned into it. He was feeling pretty stupid not to have let her drive him.

"You know, this kind of collaboration can get kind of messy over the phone. I wouldn't be surprised if personal contact isn't going to be required. Might have to write that into the contract."

"I'm confident that you'll do whatever it takes to protect us, Humphrey." He nodded, yes, he would, but how did she know that? Reluctantly he had turned to leave. Bryna figured she could watch him indefinitely so she forced her attention away from him. Out of the corner of his eye Humphrey thought he saw Bryna skipping. Or did he?

The End